(signature) Linda K. Rodante

Looking For Justice

*Christian Contemporary Romance
with Suspense*

Linda K. Rodante

LONE MESA PUBLISHING
www.lonemesapublishing.com

Looking for Justice
ISBN: 978-0692498675

Unless otherwise noted, Scripture quotations are taken from the HOLY BIBLE, NEW INTERNATIONAL VERSION, Copyright 1973, 1978, 1984, by International Bible Society. Use by permission of Zondervan. All rights reserved.

A heartfelt "thank you" goes to so many!

To:

The Word Weavers critique group of Tampa, special thank you to Sheryl Young, Janis Powell, and Sharron Cosby. I could not have done this without every one of you!

Becky Zuch, friend and beta reader, and patient listener and constant encourager.

Sue Wayne, my boss at Trinity College who always let me off for whatever writer's conference was upcoming, and for her encouragement.

Kathy Blackwell, friend, critiquer, and beta reader.

Members of Highest Praise Family Church in Tarpon Springs for reading my first manuscripts and encouraging me.

The whole Christian Indie Author Facebook group. Too many to list, but you know who you are.

Teri Burns, editor at Lone Mesa Publishing, for doing the impossible and bringing all my ideas and the needs of this manuscript together.

To:

Varina Denman, friend, encourager and author of *Jaded.*

Kathi Macias, multi-published author, encourager and fellow laborer against human trafficking.

Debby Tisdale Mayne, multi-published author, friend, and encourager.

Jessica Kirkland, agent with Blythe Daniel Agency, for her patience and encouragement.

To:

ACFW (American Christian Fiction Writers) and all the good people, information and conferences, for those that judged my contest entries and for their critiques.

Cec Murphy's scholarship to Florida Christian Writer's Conference, and to his assistant, Twila Belk who encouraged me to submit to Cec's anthology, *I Believe in Healing.*

To:

Donnie Whittemore, former Tampa Sheriff's Deputy and former Lt. Col in the Army Reserves, for his answers to numerous questions over the years.*

Cpl. Alan Wilkett with the Pasco County Sheriff's Department for his work against Human Trafficking and his answers to questions (many he never knew had to do with my writing ☺).*

Mark Mynheir, retired police officer, Palm Bay Police Department, former SWAT team member, and multi-published author, for his encouragement and help with police procedures. *

To:

The Amputee OT Blog and videos and many others that I studied, researched, and sent queries to about BKA, its effects, pain, limitations and also new freedom with the new prostheses available today.

To:

My husband, Frank, for financial support and encouragement in what proved a longer endeavor than either of us foresaw.

Both my sons, Justin and Matthew Rodante for their encouragement and patience, and to my daughter-in-law, Melissa, for her expertise on victims of abuse and the court system.*

My niece, Mindy Jaques, for her help with how paramedics handle situations.*

To:

Elaine Knadle (deceased), my mother, for her undying and enthusiastic love of Jesus and demonstration of His miracles while in missionary work and service to Him.

Wes Knadle (deceased), my dad, for giving me my first typewriter (when such things were the main means of writing) when I was 12, and by so doing, encouraging me to keep on keeping on.

And to the Lord Jesus Christ for sustaining me, training me, loving me through my life and giving me the ability to write. May the words of my mouth (and computer) and the meditation of my heart be acceptable to you, my Lord and my God.

* Any fault with police, court, paramedic procedures, etc., are strictly mine and not those of others (between not fully understanding the direction I was given or taking "poetic" license and stretching what was real to fit the story).

Chapter 1

Alexis Jergenson shoved open the door to the administration building of Appalachian Christian College and sprinted toward the stairwell. She'd left behind five years as a prosecuting attorney, and now faced her first day of class as *Professor* Jergenson.

Setting a precedent for tardiness had not entered her morning plans. The drive from her condominium to the college usually took twenty minutes, except for this morning's traffic gridlock caused by a four-car accident.

Gripping her purse in one hand and the handle of her briefcase in the other, Alexis took the short flight of stairs two at a time. As she rounded the corner to the second floor landing, she crashed into a man coming from the other direction. Her purse and case flew from her hands.

He rocked backward and seized the handrail.

Alexis grabbed at his jacket to steady herself, but only managed to yank free his perilous one-handed grip. They stumbled backward and fell. His elbow gouged her side, a hand smashed her cheek, and the hard steps slammed against her shoulder and hip.

They hit bottom, and he rolled past her. Alexis groaned and didn't move.

Feet pounded in their direction, and high, excited voices filled the air. Alexis straightened her legs, rolled to her side, and sat up. She did a quick inventory. *Nothing broken.* She tugged at her skirt. Heat rose in her face.

Beside her, the man groaned, and with an awkward movement, pushed himself into a sitting position.

"Professor Stephens!" A female student stopped beside him. "Are you okay?"

Another student leaned over Alexis, but the babble of questions and comments from the growing crowd drowned his words.

"Luke!" A man's voice broke through the chatter. "What happened?"

Glancing up, Alexis recognized Don Jacobs, an English professor. He bent over Luke Stephens and offered a hand.

The other man shook his head, his hands slipped to his knee and did a quick examination. "Give me a minute."

"Professor Jergenson?" The academic dean, Cliff Smithfield, stepped into her line of vision. "Don't move. My wife is the campus nurse. She'll be here any minute."

Gingerly, Alexis stretched one leg then the other. She rolled her head. No sharp pains. "I think I'm okay."

"You took quite a tumble. Wait until Linda gets here."

"Really, I'm okay. Just bruised."

She started to stand, and he reached to help her. Her legs wavered. The staff member next to her put a hand out, also. Alexis managed a smile, straightened and settled her feet under her.

"Thank you. I'm okay now." She tugged at her skirt again, ran shaky hands over her upswept hair, and glanced at the man on the floor. She'd recognized him, of course, right before slamming into him.

"Professor Stephens, are you okay? Is your knee hurt?"

Green eyes shifted her way, but he didn't answer, just climbed stiffly to his feet. The female student beside him put a hand forward but drew it back.

"Luke?" Don Jacob's inquiry held insistence.

"I'm fine." Luke Stephens transferred his gaze to Alexis. "And you?"

The roughness of his voice surprised her. Had the fall caused an injury? She waved a hand. "No, I'm good. Bruised is all. But are you—" A hand settled on her arm, and she glanced around to find a woman in a pair of blue scrubs standing next to her.

"Hi. I'm Linda. The nurse. Someone told me you had a fall." Her eyes focused on Luke. "You, too?"

"Both of us." Alexis touched a spot above her right ear and forced herself not to wince. "But I've been told I'm hard-headed. That's a plus today."

"Well, why don't you come to my office? Let's give this a few minutes and see how you feel. We need to do an incident report, anyway."

Alexis shifted her gaze to the floor. Her purse was here somewhere as well as the briefcase. "I'd like to make my class first. I'll come by later."

"You're sure?" When Alexis nodded, the woman's glance went to Luke.

He dipped his head. "I'll do that, too, Linda."

Alexis straightened her jacket. The heat from her face hadn't dissipated. So much for starting her class with dignity.

"All right. I'll expect to see you both later. If you have any dizziness or any other problems, come immediately or send a student to fetch me."

The academic dean cleared his throat. "Okay, everyone. Give Professor Jergenson and Professor Stephens some room. Everything's okay. Classes have started. Don't be late."

With a rumble of conversation, the students dispersed.

"I don't think we'll have to hurry to either of those classes," a student said. Another person laughed and agreed.

"Hush!" A female voice rose over the laughter. "Professor Stephens could have been hurt."

Alexis gave a quick smile and glanced at the man. He had an admirer. Not surprising. Solid build, those startling green eyes, and young—at least in this circle of academia.

The Dean nodded. "Well, come see Linda later. In the

meantime, if either of you needs to leave class, don't hesitate to call me. I'll substitute if I have to."

"Me, too." Don ricocheted a look between Alexis and Luke.

Luke met it with a wry smile. "And my students would love that. You could bring another python to class like you did last semester."

Alexis arched a brow. "A python?"

Don chuckled. "You have to get their attention somehow. Okay. I'm off to class, but keep my offer in mind." He hustled down the hall. The Dean and his wife headed back in the opposite direction.

Alexis shifted to face Luke. "I am sorry. I was running. I was late. I shouldn't..." She stopped.

Those intense eyes, their color set off by the navy blue suit he wore, had lost their amusement and narrowed as he looked at her. With her heels, she was close to his height, but five foot eight was tall for a woman. That same height gave her an edge in the courtroom, and from the vibes coming from Luke Stephens, she might need help here, too.

Her guilt turned defensive as they stared at each other. She dropped her gaze from his and looked again for her bags. Well, she had tried to apologize.

"We usually tell the *students* not to run up the stairs."

The man's words caused her hands to tighten as she grabbed her purse and case. She straightened. "Oh?"

A student raced past them and disappeared up the stairs. His pounding feet echoed back down the hall. Alexis gritted her teeth. Wonderful. As if the man needed an exclamation point to his sentence.

He cleared his throat. "For their safety, of course."

"Of course."

He was just as irritating as she remembered. For some reason, the man had taken an instant dislike to her at the faculty and staff meeting three weeks ago. Later, she'd told herself she'd imagined it. As two of the youngest members on staff, she and Luke Stephens should be allies. Not that she didn't realize and admire the scope of intelligence around her, but the age of her colleagues here compared to those in Atlanta had disconcerted her.

She tilted her head. "I'll remember that."

"Good."

She narrowed her eyes at the word, and the twitch of his mouth sent a ripple of heat through her. If he thought this was amusing… But he just gave a nod and followed Don down the hall.

Alexis stared after him. Ignore the man. You've faced worse. She settled her purse under her arm. Her students couldn't be as unfriendly as Luke Stephens and not nearly as intimidating as a hostile judge.

She mounted the stairs again. At a walk.

Chapter 2

"Come on." Alexis made a kissing sound with her mouth, but he didn't move. Instead, he watched her with distrust, muscles tightened across his chest, stance rigid. She took a deep breath. He was gorgeous. Ah, yes, gorgeous.

She put out her hand.

He shook his head, the chestnut mane flying from the thick neck, nostrils flaring.

"Oh, you...beauty."

She flattened her palm and watched the horse's eyes shift. Neither moved for a moment, but just as she was about to drop her hand, the powerful neck stretched, inching forward. Soft lips brushed her palm but found nothing. He stomped and flipped his head.

Alexis gave a quiet laugh. The ride out into the country after classes today had paid off. Her first week finished, she had craved the distraction of something beautiful, totally unrelated to teaching. Approaching Don with camera held high, she asked where to go to get pictures of the fall foliage. She envisioned the pictures blown up and mounted on the walls of her condo. He'd grinned and directed her out this long, winding road that dipped and climbed at regular intervals.

Her gaze slid to her red Jaguar parked on the other side of the fence. When she spied the stallion galloping along its perimeter, she wrenched the wheel, zipped the car to a stop on the tiny shoulder and climbed through barbed wire. Of course, she'd seen the No Trespassing sign, but beauty like this couldn't be ignored; the sign could.

"Come on, boy." She clicked her tongue. "I have carrots in the car. Really." And not because she'd expected to find a horse, but because since moving from Atlanta to Tennessee, she'd fought off loneliness by eating her way through an abundant supply of Theo Classic Chocolate bars. Even organic, Fair Trade chocolate had calories.

She bent, shoved a strand of wire up and eased a leg between it and the second strand, holding her camera close to her chest. Her jeans caught on one of the barbs, and she unhooked it before sliding her whole body through. She cast a backward glance at the horse. Her tongue made more clicking noises as she eased open the car door.

"Stay here, big boy."

Alexis grabbed a couple of baby carrots from the bag on the front seat and turned back. The wind lifted the stallion's mane, and the late afternoon sun shot waves of light through it.

Like tongues of fire. Magnificent. She lifted the small Canon camera that she'd slung around her neck. Now here was a picture...

A whistle came from somewhere over the hill, and the horse shifted.

"Wait, darling, wait." Letting the camera drop back into place around her neck, she stuck out her hand, palm flat, balancing the carrots. The animal eyed it. Alexis made kissing sounds again. "Come on. It's good. I'm not teasing now."

The soft lips crossed her palm, and the carrots disappeared. A quick crunch followed, then another. A stray piece dropped from his mouth. She reached up and rubbed his nose.

Years had passed since she'd ridden. Her parents had thought it would help...

The wind whipped her hair, and she lifted her head, studying the skies. Dark clouds bunched and grew above them. She looked back to see the horse's head inching over the wire.

Grinning, she flat-handed another carrot his way. "Here you go, boy."

Leaves spun past them, and she scrutinized a stand of nearby trees. Sassafras, sweet gum, and hickory sent swirls of yellows, golds and reds their way. She brushed her hand down the side of her jeans, pulled her phone out and began videotaping–the horse, the trees, leaves falling like rain.

To the right, the ground dropped away, and past the trees, the farmland descended to a small road. On this side, a fence hemmed in the land; beyond it, flat pasture stretched.

Wind whipped her hair across the phone. She grabbed the long strands with one hand, holding it back, and peered through the lens again. Leaves tumbled and spun past her vision. *Okay.* This was what she drove out here to see– autumn and all its glory.

A whistle brought her head around and the horse's head up.

She'd heard it before, but it hadn't registered. A rough voice called a name she couldn't understand.

"Here, boy, take it." She offered the last carrot.

The call came a second time – impatient, rough. *Uh oh.*

The third whistle was closer, louder.

"Shoo." Alexis waved him away, but he didn't move. "Go. Take off." She put a hand on his neck and shoved. "Don't get me in trouble. Some people are protective of their property."

She glanced at the No Trespassing sign. At least she stood on the correct side of the fence now.

To her left, at the top of the rise, a silhouette appeared. The person stopped and looked down at them. The stance, the hat, and thick jacket marked him as male. Alexis pulled her shoulders back and stared, narrowing her eyes to see him better.

Dark clouds had scurried from the west and banked above him, forcing the sun to shoot rays of light through their darkness. A flicker of caution leapt through her–a familiar feeling, never far away. She started to edge back to the car but stopped.

Don't be paranoid.

A bridle or halter hung from the man's shoulder, and when he started forward, she noticed the limp. Her watchfulness dropped ten degrees. Coming downhill would be hard. She eyed the sign again and stifled the desire to grab the horse's mane and lead him uphill. That move might not be appreciated.

The stallion stood still a moment longer before whinnying and trotting uphill. When the horse approached, the man reached out and rubbed a hand down his nose. He pulled a large carrot from the coat's pocket. The horse chomped and slobbered, and a minute later, the man slipped the bit between the horse's teeth and another part of the bridle over his head. His hand ran along the neck, patting again. Words spoken in an affectionate undertone reached her ears before he lifted his head to look her way.

Recognition sent a sharp jolt through her nervous system.

He came the rest of the way down the short hill, leading the horse, and stopped in front of her. Stormy green eyes met hers. Neither spoke. Jacket, jeans, and boots transformed him from the college professor she'd knocked down on Monday into a cowboy.

He hadn't been happy then; he wasn't now. She vacillated between walking to her car and holding her ground.

Luke tipped the Stetson back on his head and broke the silence. "Anyone ever tell you that feeding someone else's livestock is off-limits?"

Alexis cast a look at the stallion whose lips still evidenced slivers of orange veggies. From her carrots or his? Either way, she was busted. He must have noticed hers before feeding the horse himself. But whatever compassion she'd had while watching him walk downhill vanished.

"That's the first thing you've got to say to me? Not hello or how are you, fellow professor?"

"My first thought was, have you knocked anyone else down lately?" A half-smile appeared for an instant, but it disappeared; and he warded off her response with a lifted hand. "And my second was did you track me down to apologize?"

"Apologize?" Her voice rose. "I apologized already or tried to. Why would I—" She remembered his sharp, indrawn breath from that morning. That combined with his limp today meant something serious. Five days had passed.

A gust of wind sent leaves swirling between them. She hadn't seen him again this week. He taught Bible and business classes. Business classes were held in the Quad building, but students packed his Bible classes down from her office on the administration building's second floor. She'd recognized his voice as it drifted into her office that first afternoon and every afternoon since. Her free time coincided with his class, but he never came past her office. She assumed he disappeared down the back stairwell afterward.

She crossed her arms and lifted her chin. "I had no idea you lived here. Don sent me this way when I asked where to get pictures of the trees, the leaves. When I saw the horse, I had to stop. I... He's beautiful. But I'm sorry if the fall on Monday hurt your leg."

"The leg is fine." The words contained an edge that let her know the discussion had ended.

Okay. Wonderful. So, he didn't want to talk about it.

A car zipped past, and she realized she hadn't seen or heard another car since she'd stopped. She stepped back from the fence and away from him. The man was disagreeable, and being alone with most men made her uncomfortable. So many had that predatory look, letting their eyes slide over her like she was livestock on display. It didn't matter what she wore – business suits for the courtroom, modest dresses for evening, a pair of jeans and loose shirt to run to the store – men were predators.

Yet, Luke's deep-set eyes had never left hers. His clenched jaw reflected some strong emotion, though. As a lawyer, she'd learned to read faces. So, what was she seeing now? Before she could decide, he grabbed a handful of the stallion's mane and threw himself forward onto its back. The horse circled and stomped.

Luke straightened, pulled on the reins and looked down at her. A stab of lightning lit the sky behind him. "You'd better head into town. We're going to have a gully-washer, and the roads flood around here."

She looked past him. Heavy clouds packed the sky, and the wind bent the trees to his right.

He nodded toward her car then turned the horse. "That Jag won't make it far on flooded roads. Good evening, Miss Jergenson."

Alexis watched until they disappeared over the rise. *Into the sunset. Yeah, so apropos.*

She climbed into the Jag and turned it back toward town. The man's scowl from the moment of introduction at the staff and faculty retreat until now made her wonder if he didn't like the idea of pre-law classes being offered at a Bible college.

During the job interview, Cliff, as academic dean, mentioned the opposition that rose when he first advanced the idea. With all the challenges directed at Christian beliefs these days, he told her, a number of students had applied to law school. Offering preparatory classes would be a win-win situation – good for the college, good for the students. But not everyone agreed.

She pressed her lips together. Well, whatever the reason, she was persona non grata in Luke Stephens' life.

Rain splattered her windshield. She flipped on the wipers and glanced at her GPS. A white Honda Accord flew past going in the other direction. Glancing in the rearview mirror, she saw the car's red brake lights flash, and it swerved on the wet cement. She wrenched her attention back to the road. The drops grew in size and intensity. She flipped the wipers to high speed.

On the other hand, maybe he had discovered her secret – that she wasn't a Christian. Yet, the Dean said the President agreed on her hire. She understood their desperation. They'd spent money advertising pre-law classes then four weeks before the semester started, the professor they hired backed out. Alexis had received a call from half-way around the world informing her of the opening. Her sister-in-law had patched a call through from some tiny village in Indonesia to tell Alexis she needed to apply. She'd never learned how her sister-in-law knew of the opening, but the timing was right. Her desire to leave Bradley & Associates, to leave the past and the memories behind, had balanced with the need for another, different career.

Still, all the other professors were Christians. The Dean had asked her simply not to say anything; they'd assume she was, too. In a year, however, they would look to hire someone whose beliefs coincided with theirs. Fair enough.

Although her conscience tweaked her, their desperation mimicked hers. Her client's death had come as a shock and added an exclamation point to her own problems. She'd needed a new place and a new career. Perhaps then the haunting memories would ease.

Alexis squinted through the downpour and slowed. Shoulders along this part of the road didn't exist, just ditches. A line of rain pelted the windshield, dropping a gray curtain around her, obscuring her vision. She jerked and hit the brakes, sending the car into a slide. Heart pounding, she gripped the steering wheel and held tight. The car slowed and stopped. The front wheel on the passenger side hung over the ditch.

She sat a moment, insides jumping. Heat radiated throughout her. Her back wheels were on the asphalt. That was good, wasn't it? In her mind's eye, she could see the Jag flipped on its back in the ditch. She swallowed and straightened. Could she back out? She'd need to do that. Slowly. She didn't want to spin out going backward. Her dad's instructions from years ago crossed her mind. *Don't overcompensate.* The rain drummed against the roof, and her stomach quivered. Stop it. You're all right. Just get moving.

She put the car in reverse, eased on the gas. Nothing. She pushed harder on the pedal. The tires spun. Come on. Come on. A sudden bounce and the car shot backward.

She yanked her foot from the gas and let the car slide. It whirled in a circle, slowed and stopped. Her heart reacted like a light with a short in it. She took two deep breaths and lowered her head against the wheel. Where's a paper bag when you need it?

After a minute, her heart leveled; and she raised her head. The rain had eased, and she could see that the road before her dipped into a gully. The downpour had erased the asphalt and filled the ditches on either side. Luke's words came back to her, and she understood what he meant. The Jag's body hugged the ground, great when taking curves at high speeds, not good at getting through flooded roads.

The trouble with being new in town is that she didn't know alternate routes, and neither she nor her GPS had any idea what roads would be passable now. Her eyes focused on the rearview mirror again. No other cars had come this way since the white Honda, but the danger grew the longer she sat there.

Okay. She made a slow Y turn and headed back the way she came. Even Luke Stephens would shelter her until the rain stopped. Wouldn't he?

☙

Groaning, Luke backed up from the fireplace and dropped into the lounge chair. He'd been desperate enough to jump on the horse and ride back without a saddle in spite of his leg. Feeding and stalling the stallion and the two mares had eaten away more time, and the pain mounted with each passing minute.

When he got inside, he tore the bathroom cabinet apart looking for the pain meds even though he'd quit taking them some time ago. His head dropped back against the headrest.

Twice now, the woman had caused him more pain than he'd dealt with in the last year, and pain did things to him he didn't like. He'd wanted to take her head off, only God wouldn't let him. The strong rein on his spirit had choked back his words.

He took a deep breath, glad of the hand that had kept him from saying things he would regret. The woman had not meant to cause him pain. Something stirred in his soul. He opened his eyes and stared at the ceiling.

What is she doing here, Lord? Someone special to You?

Leaning down, he pulled off the boot and rolled up the left leg of his jeans. He'd overdone it. Walking as far as he did, and downhill at that, had pushed things too far. Not to mention the fall on Monday. Amazing that neither of them had suffered a broken bone or worse. God, again. He remembered her apology, the flush staining her cheeks and her indignation. His mouth curved into a smile.

Luke stretched his neck and rolled his shoulders. The room darkened around him. The rain started, a few scattered drops that grew into a thunderous cascade. Moments later, a torrent hit the roof. Luke turned his head and stared through the large window facing the front of the house. The downpour grayed and blurred the image of the huge tree outside.

Good thing he'd fed up. The stallion, the two mares, and Farley would ride this out in the barn. Maximus never liked the rain nor the thunder and lightning accompanying it, but he'd be fine in the closed stall. The dog would keep him company. The mares at the other end of the barn would be fine, too.

He opened his eyes and watched the tree outside bend and shift in the wind. The line of rain increased only to drop to nothing a moment later. Then it returned with mounting intensity. The meteorologists had predicted a series of squalls. That's why he'd gone to find Maximus.

And found her.

The lash of the wind and pounding rain filled his ears. He rolled his shoulders again. With the number of low places on the road between here and town, she'd never make it in that car. His truck sat higher, which was one of the reasons he'd bought it.

Not the main reason, of course; that had to do with starting over – after the divorce. He'd bought the truck and this house with twenty-five acres. Four years later, it felt like home. And the pain of someone who couldn't live with the "new" him had dimmed.

Or so he'd thought…until he saw Alexis Jergenson.

Lightning stabbed across the sky and jerked him back to the present. Rain pummeled the ground. How far had she made it before the storm broke? Numerous gullies and valleys made the road between here and the main highway treacherous during storms. Someone would need to rescue her.

Meeting her at the faculty retreat along with the other new faculty members had shaken him. She had reached forward to shake his hand, and the dark depths of her eyes and the way her long straight hair swung as she nodded at his introduction brought back memories he didn't want. Too much like Teresa. Too pretty. The sight of her had sent pain and anger ricocheting through him, surprising him.

Thunder rumbled. He sat forward. If the woman needed rescuing, he'd have to do it. Who else knew she was out there? He groaned and sat forward. Pain or not, he needed to find her. She'd be somewhere between his place and the bridge.

He headed to the front door, threw it open and almost collided with her.

Again.

She'd raised her hand to knock, and her hair and jacket

dripped water. She looked like foliage curling beside a waterfall, droplets clinging to her eyebrows, her eyelashes, and mouth.

Rain and wind blew into the house as they stared at each other. Lightning tore across the sky. Luke grabbed her arm and dragged her into the foyer, slamming the door behind her. She jumped and slid further into the hall.

Even dripping wet, she was still one attractive woman. And, like Teresa, she probably needed the proverbial bullwhip to beat the men off.

His jaw tightened. Pretty women were Trouble. Capital T. "You're drenching the floor."

She jerked her head around, and scooted back to the rug against the door, clutching her purse under one arm.

"Better?" she asked. Cynicism filled the word. "You were right about the rain. I've never seen it come down like that. The road flooded right in front of me. And you're right about the car, too. It won't make it through puddles the size this storm is dumping. I didn't know where to go, so I—" She stopped, eyeing him with a look he could read easily enough.

She wasn't any happier being here than he was having her. When he said nothing, her gaze shifted past him to the living area. The crackle of the flames in the fireplace reached him.

"Do...do you mind," she asked, trying to hide the shakes starting in her shoulders, "if I stay until it stops?"

He kicked himself inside. Quit being a jerk. She's wet and cold. Not every pretty woman is selfish and unfaithful.

Pushing past his reluctance, he indicated the room behind him. "Sure. The fire will warm you in no time."

Chapter 3

A lexis watched Luke slip through the door at the corner of the living area. He headed down the stairs that led to a garage and more wood. Or so he said. She tucked her purse in next to her, dropped her shoes on the floor and curled into the chair. Had she done the right thing? She shook away the niggling voice at the back of her mind. Where else could she go?

She put the towel he'd handed her aside, shook out the blanket, and tucked it around her. Her jacket rested on a chair closer to the fire, drying. The warmth and the glow from the fireplace spread across the room. The flames danced. Thick logs stacked inside looked like they'd last all night even if Luke had muttered something about needing more.

I ran him off.

He was uncomfortable around her. Why? In the courtroom, she could intimidate, but something happened to her there, when she was prosecuting a rapist, an abuser, or a violent husband. Her passion electrified her questioning and sometimes the whole courtroom. She understood that. But outside the courtroom? No. Outside the courtroom, men still had the upper hand.

She studied the closed door. Alone, Luke didn't seem to have many words, a change from the professor at the college. When she stopped outside his classroom today, he'd managed to impress her with his teaching on the first chapter of Isaiah. Not that all that Biblical talk made sense. She just knew intelligence when she heard it, and the students did, too, if their attentive looks meant anything.

So maybe they had something in common – confident in their fields, not so much in social situations.

Alexis leaned her head back against the seat's cushion. She'd keep her eyes open and leave when the rain let up. A moment later, she straightened. The flooding wouldn't go down immediately, and night had crept in since she'd left the first time. Still, she needed to get back to her own place.

Relax. Think about something else - a new life, getting away from Atlanta, from the life she'd buried herself in after law school. She'd never regret the five years as a prosecutor, but every case brought back the fear and shame she'd tried to forget. And until five months ago, she'd put off any type of decision.

Then two people had died.

She sighed, her chest tightening. No. Now was not the time for more tears. She watched the dancing shadows on the ceiling, the fire leaping and warm in the corner of her vision, and laid her head back against the chair. Her dad's death, coupled with Jennifer's murder at the hand of her abuser, had provided the needed thrust to quit her job and start over.

Yawning, she pulled the blanket closer around her. The long day, preceded by weeks of preparation, and the move to her condo, had crept into her shoulders, her arms and legs. Warmth from the fire drifted over her. Her body relaxed. Silence, except for the constant purr and spit of the blaze, encompassed her.

Luke was taking a long time. Letting go of the blanket with one hand, she gripped her purse, closed her eyes and trained her ears on the door across the room. When he started up the stairs, she would hear him.

❧

Luke settled the wood onto the floor next to the fireplace, making as little sound as possible. Alexis' head rested against the cushion, the blanket slipping halfway to the floor.

He'd stayed longer downstairs than needed, tinkering with a few things. The pantry with fresh canned corn and beans and pickles that his neighbors had given him didn't need straightening, but he'd done it anyway.

He focused on the rain outside the bay window. The storm hadn't stopped and wouldn't for a while. She wasn't getting out of here tonight. Should he wake her and let her know? Dropping off to sleep like this implied exhaustion. She was working hard and not trying to get by on her reputation as a lawyer. That was good. From what he'd heard, her teaching style, while a little unskilled, still captured the students' interest.

He listened to her quiet breathing and studied her. Dark lashes rested against delicate skin, and dark, tousled hair made her look younger than he'd first thought. But in all probability, she needed to look and act older in the courtroom to get respect. Some people would have trouble getting past her outward appearance to the inward intelligence underneath.

How long was law school? She'd be in her early thirties, maybe, younger than he by a few years.

He stepped back. What did it matter? Her age, her looks? He wasn't looking for physical beauty, anyway. He couldn't give it; he didn't want it. After Teresa, he'd made the decision to find someone plain and someone who liked to laugh. Heart trumped looks anytime.

The smell of burning wood wrinkled her nose. Alexis drew her hand across her nostrils and opened her eyes. Darkness lit by the smoldering fire jerked her heart, and her gaze flicked from one side of the room to the other. Memory flooded her, and she jolted upright.

The room was empty except for the furniture and the fire. A pillow and another blanket balanced on the overstuffed arm of a large chair next to her. She glanced around the room again then pulled the phone from her purse to check the time.

Midnight.

She'd slept for hours?

Firelight lit the far reaches of the room, but the rest of the house was dark. Where was Luke? Was he asleep, too, in one of the other rooms? Her stomach tightened, and the muscles across her shoulders did the same.

Standing, she eased toward the first doorway. She needed a bathroom, but didn't want to wake him if he slept in another room. A board squeaked. She hesitated, listening, before she glanced through the closest doorway. A kitchen. Little green lights glowed like gremlin eyes on the microwave, the coffee pot, the stove. Two doors led from it. One to the outside? Could the other be the bath?

She turned and focused on the side door that led to the stairs. Next to it was the beginning of a long hall. Definitely a bathroom down there, along with what was probably his bedroom.

So, an older model home from the layout, with some updating – the living room's wood floor, for one. In the firelight, it glowed. Still, she hesitated.

"Are you looking for the bathroom?"

She gasped, jumped, and spun around. He stood in the dark kitchen, a darker shadow against many others.

"Sorry. I didn't mean to scare you."

"You...I...well, you did." Her voice accused but her heart stammered along with her words. The firelight played over a t-shirt and flannels as he moved forward. Her feet slid backward. She couldn't see his smile, but she heard it in his next words.

"Didn't mean to scare you, but it makes us even, don't you think?"

"Makes us even?"

"Yeah, I think it does. You knocked me down on Monday,

fed my horse this afternoon; but I'll call it even."

"What?" The squeak of her voice brought the definite glint of a smile this time.

"Even." Then his head indicated the hall. "Were you looking for the bathroom? It's that way. My room's back through the kitchen. With my bath. I'm sure you don't want that."

She swallowed and told her heart to slow. She'd guessed wrong about his room. "Okay, yes. And then I should be going. It sounds like the rain has stopped."

He had started to turn back toward his room but stopped and faced her again. "No. You won't be going anywhere until morning."

Alexis straightened her shoulders. "I'll go when I feel ready."

He waited a hair's breath. "Actually, you won't. You can leave, but you won't get far in either direction. The roads are still flooded."

Her heart wasn't listening to her command. Neither were her legs. She'd told them to move away from him, but they didn't budge.

"I'm telling you the truth, you know. The flooding won't have receded."

He was right. She knew he was right. *Get hold of yourself!*

"Okay." It squeaked out.

Silence settled between them.

He stepped away from her. "You might be stuck here, but you're safe. Trust me."

"I…"

"The bathroom's down the hall, third door on the left. You can sleep on the couch or in one of the bedrooms. They both have locks." He turned and walked into the dark.

A few minutes later she settled onto the couch, bunched up the pillow, and flipped the blanket over her. The glow from the fire enticed her.

Trust him? Yeah, right. She'd only trusted two men in her life. Her father's strong, tall image hovered close, the grief still acute.

She forced a deep breath and opened her eyes. The embers glowed and cooled and flared. The flames leapt upwards.

And the second man was halfway around the world flying a little rickety plane into some snake-infested jungle. She shoved the hair back from her face. And if he ever came home again, he'd hear from her good and hard.

Chapter 4

The dream came that night. It hadn't for months, but like the physical pain that had filled his day, the dream filled his night.

The sound of the bullets occurred first, followed by the noise of flesh being torn, of screams and yells and cursing. Then the explosion. He saw the hit, his best friend thrown back from the blast, and blood everywhere. He ran forward to get him, and then he was flying backward through the air – away from Clint, away from the others on his team. The ground slammed him, and for minutes, he couldn't think or see.

He sat up in bed, sweating, the pounding of his heart as if he'd been there again. He waited for the pounding to slow, trying to push the dream and the thoughts aside, but without success.

He remembered someone grabbing him under the arms and dragging him away. He'd fought them and shouted for Clint but to no avail. Vaguely, he remembered a field medic bandaging his leg and his screams of pain as they raced him to the helicopter. Sometime during the flight, he'd passed out.

The next few days, he fought anger and bitterness and unbelief. And pain. Medication brought relief and rest, but he didn't like it.

He needed a conversation with God, the God whom he had served his whole life – as far back as he could remember, accepting his Savior at the age of six. He'd never deviated. He wouldn't now, but he wanted that conversation. He'd earned it, and he wanted to be in his right mind when it came.

≈

Alexis squinted toward the kitchen doorway. Soft light spilled from it. Something scraped across the counter, and then a chair scratched the floor. Paper rattled. She listened a few more minutes but silence reigned. Across the room, the fire had grown cold and dark. He had been right about the wood. Only he hadn't stoked the fire during the night.

She pulled her purse from under her pillow, pushed her hand inside and found her phone. *Five thirty. In the morning.*

He was up already? She started to huddle back under the blanket but knew that since he was awake, she wouldn't sleep either. Besides, she needed to get out of here. Groaning, she climbed to her feet and stumbled down the hall.

A few minutes later, she rested her shoulder against the open doorway and stared at him. He sat at the table, his hand cupping a tall coffee cup, a Bible open in front of him. The laptop next to it shone its light onto the book. He hadn't turned on the overhead light. A concession to her? The kitchen's light would have sprayed its brilliance into the living area.

He looked up and met her gaze. "Morning."

"It's still dark."

He raised a brow, and one side of his mouth lifted. "It is, but I think morning still applies."

"You're a morning person."

His smile broadened. "And you're not."

"Why is it that morning people are so smug?"

"Are we?"

Alexis frowned. How could he look so wide awake and put together? His cinnamon-brown hair caught the glow of his laptop looking as if it were still damp from a shower. The strong jaw was shaved, and the corners of his eyes crinkled at her. "You want coffee?" he asked.

She eased over to a chair, slid it out, and rested her elbows on the table, sliding her head into her hands. "I guess I need something."

"I guess you do." He stood and walked over to the counter. "You want milk and sugar? There's no fancy stuff here."

Great. "I suppose you take yours black."

"Good guess. Or is that the lawyer's powers of deduction?"

She straightened. "Are you usually sarcastic in the morning?"

He cleared his throat, set a coffee cup in front of her and went back to the counter. A moment later, he walked over with a gallon of milk and a sugar bowl. He set the milk and sugar on the table and handed her a spoon.

"Not usually. Sorry."

"I just bring it out in you. Is that it?" She poured as much milk into the cup as possible. He hadn't left much room. She added two sugars. "Obviously, I need to do something to make up for knocking you down on Monday."

He frowned at her cup then met her look. "No. Let me start over."

Start over? Was he serious? "Okay."

The side of his mouth twitched again. "Morning."

If the tendency to amusement was any indication, daybreak was his best time. She tried a smile of her own. "Morning."

He nodded, walked to the doorway, and flipped the light switch.

She squinted into the unexpected brightness. "Oh, my goodness."

"You want breakfast?"

"It's 5:30." Her stomach clenched. Besides, she didn't want him cooking for her. "No, I... How's the storm?"

He opened the refrigerator and took out eggs, cheese and a can of biscuits. "I'm going to make something for myself. You can eat or not. The storm's still with us."

"What does that mean?"

"Check the laptop. We have another line of squalls almost

on top of us. Was quiet when I got up, but if you listen, you can hear rumbling from the west."

Her coffee cup hit the table. She couldn't be stuck here. She needed to get home, needed to spend the weekend going over next week's curriculum. "What about getting home? I have a lot to do."

He cracked eggs into a bowl, grabbed the milk and poured some into it then used a fork to beat them together. "Where is your place?"

She gave him the name of the condo and the street name.

"Hmmm." The eggs went into a pan. He rapped the canned biscuits on the counter, pulled it open, and began placing them on a tray. "Streets will be flooded in town, too. But it's from here to there that will be the biggest problem. If you hadn't conked out cold last night, we could have discussed it."

Heat rose in her face. "I didn't mean to fall asleep. I didn't realize how exhausted I was." When he only nodded, she forced the next words from her throat. "Thank you for letting me stay."

"Nothing else you could do."

"I had no idea I'd be stranded all night. And today…" The unease she'd nurtured through the night fluttered inside. "I can't stay."

The metal tray slid into the oven. He stirred the eggs and turned. His brow creased. A jagged streak of lightning showed through the windows, against the dark sky. Thunder cracked. Alexis jerked and grabbed the sides of the table. She couldn't stay here.

"I can't stay, Brock. I'm sorry. It's not going to work." The cabin walls seemed to draw closer.

"Alexis." His hands caught her arms. "You can't go anywhere in this storm. We came here for a reason. Everything will be fine."

"No, I…"

He leaned forward. "Calm down. You're too uptight."

She pulled against his hold. "I told you it might not work. You knew that."

He leaned in to kiss her, but she twisted her face away. When his hands tightened, she pulled against them.

Anger flashed in his eyes. "Come on. Stop the baby stuff."

"No." She yanked free of his grasp.

Lightning struck somewhere outside the cabin. "You're stuck here, my girl. Whether you like it or not."

They'd brought her car because she wanted to feel in control, and now she knew why. Grabbing her purse, she started for the door.

"Alexis, stop!"

As she reached the door, his hand closed on her arm and jerked her around.

"Let go, Brock. I'm not staying."

"You think I've put in all this time with you for nothing?"

All the warnings that she'd ignored during his sweet talking the week before leapt like flames inside her. "I'm leaving. Now."

His other hand clamped over her arm, and he dragged her against him. "You aren't going anywhere, you hear me? You're not going anywhere."

"You aren't going anywhere," Luke said.

His voice shocked her back to the present and ratcheted up the fear inside. She stood and stepped away from him.

A puzzled expression crossed his face before he turned back to the stove. "Between here and town are numerous low places. You'll never get the Jag through. Believe me."

Alexis willed her mind to clear. She stared at the back of Luke's head.

He took a bag of shredded cheese and added some to the pan. "I checked the weather as soon as I got up and saw the reports of flooding." His voice came over his shoulder. "If it stops raining by midmorning, you might make it out by late afternoon. If you can't get the Jag out, I'll take you home in my truck."

She eased toward the doorway. "I...I need my purse. My phone."

He turned from the stove, studying her. "Go ahead. Things are almost done here. You'll feel better if you eat. You had nothing last night."

She rotated and walked into the living area and grabbed her purse. Thunder rolled again; lightning flashed. She glanced outside. The night had lightened. Daylight would bring relief.

Although, it had brought no relief the other time.

She'd crept out of the cabin when Brock fell asleep, after his self-preservation speech that what had happened was what she wanted, what she planned when she agreed to come for the weekend.

The mountain road proved so dangerous that she had stopped not far from the cabin and waited for full daylight, knowing that daylight could not change what happened and that she'd never be the same.

"Come eat." Luke's voice drifted from the kitchen. "My cooking's not that bad. And I think I remember some flavored creamer, after all. My mother brought it when she was here last. Ruined her coffee the same way you do."

She stared at the doorway. She'd been stupid last time, but she hadn't been since and wouldn't start now.

Luke stepped into view. He studied her a moment then held up a carton. "Hazelnut. The date's okay. Join me?"

Alexis swallowed, pulled a chocolate bar from her purse and waved it at him. "What you meant to say, obviously, was that your mother has good taste just like I do." She took a deep breath and eased in his direction.

He stepped back toward the stove just as the buzzer sounded.

&

Luke set the egg and cheese biscuit in front of her alongside the hazelnut creamer. He didn't know what had spooked her, but the look in her eyes a minute ago mirrored Maximus' on a bad day. The stallion hated storms. In fact, he would have checked on the horse before breakfast if Alexis had slept longer.

Lord, give this woman peace. I don't know what she's afraid of, but let her know I'm no threat to her.

They ate in silence, the storm moving over them, lending its own voice to the meal. As they finished and Luke poured his second mug of coffee, it grew quiet outside.

She hadn't asked for more coffee, and he was thankful for that. He was having trouble watching her drink the first. After she'd taken a few sips, she'd put half the chocolate bar into her coffee and more milk. His stomach had revolted

Alexis stood, walked to the sink and rinsed her dish. "Are storms always this violent here?" She looked down at the cabinets.

"Leave it in the sink. I never use the dishwasher. Just have one dish, one pan most of the time." He rose, too.

Alexis moved back. He pretended not to notice that she gave him a wide arc. Her nervousness last night was understandable, but for a short time this morning, she appeared relaxed. What had scared her?

"Over the last few years, we've had more of these destructive-type storms." He put his own dish in the sink and picked up his head, listening. What had he heard?

"I could do without—"

He held up a hand. "Wait a minute, will you?"

"What?"

"Be quiet." He moved to the back door and opened it, cocked his head and listened. The barking was clear now. Farley. He didn't like the tone. "Stay here. I need to check the barn."

"You...what?"

Not answering, he slipped out the door, strode across the deck and down the walk to the barn. He dodged the puddles. Farley's barking rose in determined alarm. When he got to the doors, he heard the horses, too. He lifted the beam and swung the doors wide.

At the far end of the barn, the two mares stomped and stretched their heads over the bottom doors of their stalls. They looked agitated, but he swung his gaze to the closed stall on his left. Farley's barking almost drowned Maximus' snorting and pawing.

The dog was supposed to keep the stallion calm during storms. Why was he making such a ruckus?

Luke unlatched the top door and swung it wide. Maximus threw his head up, stamped and made a high-pitched whinny. As he eyed the horse, Farley jumped at the open half-door and tried to crawl over.

"Down, boy, down. Be quiet." He patted the dog's head and studied Max. "What's up? You want out?" He lifted the bar from the bottom door, and the dog squeezed through, barking again. Luke slipped inside. The horse swung his head and stomped with short nervous movements. "What's the problem? The storm upset—"

The hole behind the horse was three feet from the floor and would measure just bigger than a horse's hoof. Luke's head whipped back to Max. Hay covered the back hooves but bright, red blood painted the straw around his left leg.

"Max." He inched forward, put a palm on the stallion's flank and eased his hand down the back leg. The horse shifted away from him. "Hold on, boy. Let me look." He slipped his hand down the leg again. Blood coated the thick fur.

The horse snorted, and Luke grabbed the leg, lifting it. He jumped aside as Max kicked out, hitting the side of the barn again. Luke moved to his head.

"Calm down, boy. You're okay. Calm down."

"Anything I can do?"

Luke looked over the half gate. Alexis stood at the barn door, rubbing Farley's ears. He frowned. Usually Farley was a nipper and protective, but she'd made it to the barn without the dog setting up an alarm. And this was just what he needed – both a guest and a horse that required attention.

"Thanks, but I need a vet." One of the mares neighed, and he shot a glance that way. "And I need to get the mares out. They're agitated enough. I don't want another injury."

Her expression changed, and she walked to the stall door. "The stallion's injured?"

"Yes. He kicked a hole in the outside wall. Injured his leg. Lot of blood, but I can't see what's what." He let himself out the door. "Don't get too close. He's jumpy."

She backed up a foot. *A foot.* He didn't have time to watch out for her.

"You'd better wait in the house. I've—"

"I know horses." She cut him off. "I had one of my own, and I worked at a stable – cleaning, feeding, washing, all the usual stuff. I can get the mares out for you while you call the vet. Where do you want them?"

He hesitated, eyeing her. She was tall, looked strong, like she worked out, and if she knew horses…"You're sure?"

"Just show me where you want them."

He eyed her again, undecided. Her previous nervousness had disappeared. She seemed calm and in control.

"I can handle them. Trust me." She said it with a half-smile, accenting the last two words.

He missed the meaning she was trying to convey, but he could use the help. "Okay."

He pointed at the gate a short distance from the barn. His one-second view of Max's leg had given him no idea how bad the injury was. He needed to make that call and get back. He caved to the need.

"I'll open the gate for you on the way back to the house. I left my phone there."

"The lead rope?"

"Hanging next to the stalls. Look, take the black one out first. That's Mandy. Make sure you close the gate after you put her in the field. Come back for Sandy. She's blind. She doesn't go into the field without Mandy."

Alexis' focus switched from the horses to him. "She's blind?"

"Yeah. I went to buy a horse, got stuck with two. They wouldn't separate them." He saw a glint of amusement in her eyes and frowned. "Mandy's a great horse when I have someone else who wants to ride. Sandy's not bad either as long as there's a trail and Mandy leads."

The woman's brows rose. She angled away from him heading toward the mares. "And you're a pushover."

She said it under her breath, but he heard it and scowled. Maybe at the time, but it was too soon after the divorce; and somehow the thought of tearing two other beings apart – horses or not – hadn't sat well with him. He'd bought them both.

He glanced again at Max before making a run for the house. Farley didn't follow as usual. He looked around before going in the back door. Alexis was leading Mandy to the gate, and the Blue Heeler was loping beside her, head up, grinning. Luke shook his head and went to get his phone.

Chapter 5

Friday afternoon, and the tiredness creeping over her felt good. She'd made it through week two. A smile played across her face.

She propped herself against the four-foot retaining wall of the administration building that overlooked the building's main entry. She liked the view from this second-floor area, liked the large windows that fronted the building. Outside, a carpet of grass stretched to a line of crimson and yellow trees. Beyond those, the mountains warmed a darkening sky. Below and to the right, students, faculty and staff exited the building toward the college's main parking lot.

Alexis would leave, too, but, right now, she waited here for a purpose. Luke had followed her halfway home Saturday evening just to make sure the roads were passable. She hadn't seen him but briefly since, and she had no idea how Maximus was doing. Taking the other horses out to the field should have earned her some points, but if it did, she couldn't tell. He hadn't stopped by to say hello much less give her an update on the horse. The man had grunted the one time they'd passed in the hall. Other than that, he had returned her wave from the parking lot this morning. That's it. As she'd suspected, his social skills rated right up there with her own. And those were a joke.

When she tried hurrying to catch up with him this morning, she'd dropped the six books she carried; and by the time she gathered them again, he had disappeared through the front doors. Yeah, an e-reader would be easier, but books could be lent to students in a way e-readers could not.

Her waiting this afternoon, though, looked worthless. He must have left earlier or slipped down the backstairs, as he often did.

"Who in this school has the money to drive a Jaguar, Rachel?" Professor Jacobs' voice carried to the second floor where she stood.

"I think it belongs to Professor Jergenson."

Alexis leaned over the wall and glanced down. Don propped himself against the receptionist's desk. She admired the distinction of his raven hair. A nice looking man that had made her feel welcome. Unlike some others.

"You think?" Don asked. "Well, you might be right. She's a lawyer, after all."

Cliff Smithfield walked past, heading out. The college President, Jim Edwards, was at his side. "Yes, she is. It certainly classes up the parking lot."

"It does." Don straightened his tie. "Wonder how fast that thing goes."

"A Jag? Oh, they're fast. Ask her for a ride." The President pushed the outside door open and walked out.

"Maybe I will."

Alexis leaned over to add her own content, but her arm was caught and someone pulled her around. She glanced up to see Luke frowning at her. She glared at his hand on her arm and tugged herself free. As much as she'd sought to see him, she wasn't going to be man-handled by anyone.

She started to say something when she noticed the female student behind him.

"Do you have a few moments?" he asked.

Alexis recognized the girl from one of her classes. Her blue eyes and blond ponytail accented an attractive face. Alexis eyed the black smudges under her eyes and the way her arms clasped her purse to her midsection.

"Sure." She smiled at the girl. "Jessica, right? Did you need something?"

The student's gaze went to Luke and when he nodded, her

eyes focused on Alexis. "I...Professor Stephens thinks I should talk with you."

Alexis gave Luke a quick look. He inclined his head, and she moved further away from the wall. Words not only carried up to the second floor but down to the first. "Why don't we go to my office?"

She led the way. The girl motioned Luke to follow.

Alexis sat at her desk. The other two settled in the chairs across from her. Luke leaned back and crossed an ankle over a knee as if to take himself out of the discussion.

Alexis smiled. "How can I help you, Jessica?"

The girl's gaze slid Luke's way again before focusing on Alexis. "I have...a problem."

"Oh?"

"I live with my mother and her boyfriend."

Alexis added her own nod. Whatever this student told her would bring no surprises. Students came to the Christian college, like any other college, from all sorts of backgrounds.

"My mother's boyfriend, Leland, moved in with us a few months ago. I...I knew he was trouble from the start. You know how you just know?" When Alexis indicated agreement, Jessica swallowed and continued. "I tried to tell mom, but she wouldn't listen. Leland's a bum. He sits home all day and drinks beer and watches TV while Mom works."

Alexis' lips tightened. She'd dealt with too many men like that. Her days in court were full of them. She could guess what was coming next.

Jessica glanced again at Luke. He inclined his head but said nothing. The girl's posture shifted. She hunched forward, drawing in on herself.

"He...he was always coming on to me when mom wasn't there. I hated it." Her voice dropped. "Then one day, he tried to kiss me. I...hit him, scratched him. I thought if Mom sees this and asks, I can finally tell her; and we could get rid of this jerk. But it made him mad and...he...raped me."

In her lap, Alexis' fists clenched. As usual, she toned down her own response. She'd learned a long time ago that too much emotion could scare victims, and what the girl needed now was understanding and validation.

She leaned forward. "I am so sorry, Jessica. This should never happen to anyone. Don't blame yourself."

The girl's eyes focused on Luke. "That's what Professor Stephens said."

Alexis met Luke's glance. Good thing he'd brought Jessica to talk with her. The girl could develop a dependency on him or even, at some point, find herself romantically attracted to him. Counseling, whether professional or not, had definite risks, not what any of them needed at this point.

"Did you tell your mom or the police?"

Jessica shook her head. "No. I...I couldn't. Leland said he would tell everyone I initiated it if I told anyone. That Mom was already suspicious...of me." Her voice rose. "He said she would hate me, might even throw me out."

Alexis watched the tears form in the girl's eyes and clamped down on her anger. The story was so typical, repeated hundreds of times a year.

"Did you think he might be lying about your mom, so that you wouldn't say anything?"

"Yes. I yelled at him. I told him Mom would never believe him. But he shook me so hard. He...he scared me. And then he said he'd told Mom and our neighbors how I was after him. That everybody already knew I was trying to seduce him." Her voice broke.

Alexis knew she had to ask the question but lowered her voice, moderated it. "And had you?"

"No! I can't stand him!"

Luke touched her arm. "It's all right, Jessica. Alexis...Professor Jergenson has to ask."

Alexis nodded. "He's right. I have to ask. When did this happen?"

"This summer. Before school started."

She put her elbows on the desk, entwined her fingers and

concentrated on the girl. "Jessica, why are you telling us now?"

"I'm...pregnant."

A couple of quiet moments passed before Alexis leaned back in the chair. Luke, though, did not move. Instead, his lips thinned.

"You're sure? You did a test?"

"Yes, I...I went to that pregnancy center. The Christian one where the tests are free. They said they'd help me if I needed it. They...they encouraged me to have the baby, not to get an abortion."

"And have you decided what you're going to do?"

"Well, of course. I mean...I have to have it – the baby. Don't I?"

Alexis hesitated. She knew enough to realize that even at a Christian college, some girls were not only sexually active, but some had already had abortions.

"Jessica, you have to decide that for yourself."

Luke shifted in his chair. Alexis sent him a quick glance. He might very well have strong feelings about it. Most people did – one way or the other. "You and your beliefs and what you can live with. There is another option, you know."

"Are you talking about adoption? They mentioned that at the pregnancy center. I could never do that."

"If you aren't in a position to bring up a child, it can be a very good option. I've known girls who did, and it ended well. Most adoptions these days are open adoptions. That means you can pick the parents from a group presented to you, maybe that can't have children of their own; and you can see the baby as he or she grows." Alexis waved her hands. "But nothing has to be decided this minute. You can think about it. Did you tell the people at the pregnancy center what happened?"

"No. I just let them think I had a boyfriend. It wouldn't have made a difference to them, you know. Life...life is important."

Alexis moved her head in concurrence. One of the things where she found herself in agreement with these Christians was that life was important – everyone's life. She'd dealt with too many people who thought no life was important but their own.

"Jessica, what do you want now? What did you want from Professor Stephens? What do you want from me?"

Jessica's head turned Luke's way. "I...I..."

When she stumbled, Luke spoke. "She didn't approach me. I noticed how upset she was and asked her to stay after class." He smiled at the girl. "I'm not sure she would have said anything if I hadn't pushed."

"I...I needed to talk to someone. I just didn't know who."

"You haven't told anyone else?"

"No. I just wanted it to go away. I've never been alone with Leland again. I made sure of that. No matter what. But then..."

"Then you found out you were pregnant."

"Yes." The girl's face crumbled. "What am I going to do? And what about school? The Dean will dismiss me if he finds out."

Alexis lifted questioning eyes to Luke. When his eyes gave assent, she wanted to roll hers. So, they'd penalize the girl because she was raped?

Luke bent his head toward the girl. "I'm sure Professor Jergenson would go with you to talk with the Dean. The rules of no smoking, no drugs, no co-habitation, etcetera are to show that our lives are dedicated to Christ, that we don't live like the world; but this is different."

"So true." Alexis' voice amped. "And, of course, I'll go with you. In the meantime, do you want to press charges?"

The girl's head dropped. "I don't know what to do. Leland will say I'm lying, and how will I prove differently?"

Alexis steepled her hands. "You're pregnant. They will be able to do a DNA match to prove the child is his. He won't be able to deny that."

"Oh! I didn't think about that." Excitement filled her face for a few moments only to crumple. "But we'd have to go to court, right? And he'd just say I was lying about the rape. I...I don't know."

If the girl had called the police at the time, if she hadn't waited...but that was so easy to say. The police interrogation and the hospital evidence collection would have made her feel dirty and alone. Jessica had kept it to herself for a reason – the fear, the embarrassment, and the sense of violation had compounded to make her feel isolated and ashamed.

Alexis swallowed. The girl's obvious distress tugged at her. Alexis stood, came around the desk and leaned down to hug her.

"Jessica." Her voice was hoarse. "You are a wonderful person. This will change your life, your world; but don't let it destroy you. You can go on and do great things no matter what."

Jessica hugged her back, holding tight. When the girl sniffed, Alexis let go and grabbed a tissue from the box on her desk.

"Here." She smiled, pulled back and walked around the desk again, passing Luke but not looking at him. Men usually didn't see her soft side, didn't see the emotions she struggled so hard to contain.

She took a deep breath and concentrated on the girl. "I want you to take a few days and think about a number of things. Do you want to prosecute? If so, I will be on your side. I can't practice in Tennessee, but I'll go with you to the prosecutor's office. Also, you'll need to tell your mother and close friends. You can't hide the fact that you're pregnant forever. Decide what you want to tell them."

"Okay."

"Some friends will be great; others will be judgmental. You can't get around it. And it's the ones you least expect that will support you. Others may not. You have to know that and expect it. The same, I'm sorry to say, is true of your mother. Your living situation could be affected. Do you have a friend you could stay with for a while, if needed?"

"You think my mom might throw me out like Leland said?"

"I don't know your mom or the relationship you have with her. But it's best to be prepared. If you prosecute, you might need a restraining order or Order of Protection against Leland. If you file, he will have to move. If your mother believes you, all could be good. But if not..." She let it trail off and watched the girl a moment. "None of this will be easy, but we," she glanced Luke's way and saw his head dip in agreement, "will be here for you."

Alexis picked up a card from her card holder and wrote her cell number on it. "Here, if you need me at any time, call."

"Okay."

"I mean that. In the weeks to come, you will want someone to talk with. Call me." She leaned forward again. "Jessica, I recommend counseling. You might not feel you need it, but it will help. I believe one or two of the professors here have their own counseling practices. They can help, and they will keep what you say private; or they can give you referrals for someone outside the college."

"Okay." Jessica's voice whispered.

"You don't have to do anything this minute. Take the weekend and think about it. You have a friend with whom you can spend the weekend?"

"I...I hadn't thought about that. I can spend the weekend with Rachel. That would be good." Jessica rose, her eyes downcast, and fumbled with her purse.

Alexis rose, too, and came around her desk. "You will have to tell your mom, but think about when you want to do that and make sure Leland isn't there. Keep my card handy in case you need to call. I can be there if you want."

Luke gave the girl a quick hug. Alexis did the same and watched her walk down the hall and disappear down the stairs. Her heart felt heavy. She hoped Jessica would take her advice and see a counselor. In Atlanta, she knew the right ones, had their cards on her desk, knew she could make a call; and they would work someone into their schedule for her. But here…

They stood in silence a minute before Alexis moved back to her desk and sat down. She fought the urge to put her head on her desk.

"Thank you."

Alexis focused on him. "No, thank you for bringing her."

"I had to. She needed help, and I remembered Cliff mentioning your concentration of abuse and rape cases at the faculty retreat. It seemed the right thing to do."

"I hate this, hate it when women, young girls, whoever, are taken advantage of like that."

"I could tell."

"Men are so…" She stopped herself, reined it back.

"And mothers that prefer to believe their boyfriends instead of their daughters are, too. But you're right. In today's society, men have left their first estate – knowing God, loving their families, loving and respecting others."

She stared at him, surprised and a little confused by his words. He had an odd way of talking sometimes. She frowned and stood and waved at her desk. "I need to get my things together and get home."

He walked to her door. "Thanks again. Jessica needed the help, will continue to need some."

"I'll do everything I can."

"I thought that." He stepped through the doorway. "I'll try to make sure she sees a counselor."

"That's important."

"I know." He turned to go.

"Luke."

He looked back. "Yes?"

"How is Max doing?"

His eyes crinkled at the corners. "Better. He's still in the stall for another week, except for an occasional hour or so outside in the corral. The gash was pretty deep, and he's not a good patient; but he'll be fine."

"Good. He's so beautiful."

He nodded and went down the hall. She stared after him.

Not as tall as her brother, but wider in the shoulders. Where her brother was lean, Luke was sturdy, his face mobile, not quite handsome. Interesting, though, with character. And great eyes.

She shuffled a few papers. But with a slight limp this afternoon. No limp this morning; slight limp now. So, he limped as the day wore on. Strange. He must have some other injury – more than the fact that she'd knocked him down that first morning. Ten days later, he still limped. Perhaps the fall had aggravated an old injury. And perhaps his surliness that day had something to do with that. She began to arrange papers and books for the next day's classes. So, he and his horse both nursed a bad leg.

The man had let her spend the night, made her breakfast, and followed her halfway to town that day just to make sure the Jag would make it. Responsible. She could tag that onto what she knew of him. And caring. He hadn't just dropped Jessica off, but had stayed and agreed to help as needed.

A moment later, she pushed her chair back from her desk and began to pace. What had she done? She'd moved here to get away from this, away from the emotional turmoil inside her. Yet, without thinking, she'd slid back into the role she'd played for the last five years. Her hands caught the clip in her hair and pulled it free. Her hair dropped to her shoulders, and she shoved her fingers through it. Each conviction helped. That truth had driven her through law school and into practice. But why had she agreed to help now?

She stopped and rested both hands on her desk. Because she couldn't do anything else. Grabbing her keys, her purse and her Theo Classic Chocolates, she headed toward the door. Come next week, she'd visit the District Attorney's office and put this into someone else's hands.

Chapter 6

The third Monday, and her student's excitement had waned. She had assigned last week's homework to find out who would do the work required and who just thought law was an interesting subject. If someone needed to drop out, now was the time.

The laptop screen blurred before her eyes. She rolled her head back and from side to side then stood and walked to the office doorway. The door to Luke's classroom stood open, as always. His voice resonated down the hall. She couldn't make out particular words, but the cadence and huskiness of it massaged her shoulders.

The students liked him, respected his teaching. She'd seen and heard that each day as they passed by when leaving his class. But Luke never came this way. He took the backstairs down to his other classroom and, again, when the day ended.

She positioned herself in the doorway, waiting for his class to end. Jessica hadn't shown for her class this morning nor for Luke's now. Alexis had strolled by and glanced in to make sure. Neither had the girl contacted her over the weekend. That didn't surprise her, but Alexis had expected to see her and talk with her today.

Luke's voice stopped, laughter followed, and the noise of papers and shuffling feet met her before the students began leaving. Conversation bubbled as they filed past her. Alexis smiled and nodded and waited until they disappeared. When they did, she made her way to Luke's room but stopped at the sound of a female voice inside.

Her limited view of the room did not include Luke or the

student whose voice rose even as Alexis wondered if she should leave or not.

"I don't see anything wrong with what I am wearing."

Luke replied in a low voice that she strained to hear. "You know the dress code. I'm just asking you to wear something in keeping with that."

"No one else said anything." The girl's tone challenged him.

"I'm saying something." His voice faded. The sounds of papers and books moving across the desk followed. "Remember this is a Christian college and remember who you're dressing for."

"You don't have to dress like the Church Lady to be a Christian."

"No one said you do." A trace of amusement sounded in his voice. "Look, just put a t-shirt on under the dress if you wear it again. It's not a big deal, Stephanie. It's what the other girls do. Just follow the dress code."

"Maybe I should dress like that girl, Rachel. Man, is she dowdy. Or Professor Jergenson. Wow, I wonder if that's how she dresses in the courtroom because she's not getting any attention like that."

"Professor Jergenson dresses just fine. I'm sure she doesn't want the type of attention you're talking about. A good defense or offense works better with a jury than a low-cut dress."

"Yeah, well…"

"Stephanie, I've got a few things to do. I'll see you tomorrow in class."

Alexis scooted back down the hall, slipped into her office and sat at the desk. A moment later, the girl walked past. Alexis couldn't stop herself from glancing up and taking in the dress. Colorful and swinging lose above her knees. A summer dress with spaghetti straps and a plunging front. The spaghetti straps were a "no-no" on campus much less the abundance of cleavage. No wonder…

The Church Lady? She looked like the Church Lady on that old SNL show? Her hands touched her hair. She wore it pulled up while teaching and always in court. Looking down, she studied the long-sleeved jacket and white shirt she'd put on that morning.

She knew that compared to some of the other female attorneys, her suits were modest, even plain; and yes, she wore the same clothes to class because it seemed appropriate. If you were interested in law, you needed to start thinking and dressing like a professional.

She owned a few elegant dresses, mostly worn at special occasions for her family. Her father had bought her a black lace dress a few years back to wear to a banquet in her honor – an acknowledgement from the community of her fight to stop violence against women. The dress had reminded her she could still be that attractive woman she used to see in the mirror.

A movement at the door jerked her head up. Luke leaned against the door jam. The sleeves of his shirt were rolled to his elbows, and he wore dress slacks that somehow gave the feeling of casual elegance. She focused on his shoes. No boots today, a pair of dress shoes instead. Similar to what he'd worn the first day of class but without the jacket. He looked relaxed and amused.

Alexis knew she was frowning even as she stared at him. His casual pose and the amusement didn't sit well with her. Yet, he'd defended her and the way she dressed. Did it reflect his real opinion? Well, she didn't care. People's opinions about her dress had never made a difference to her.

Her frown deepening, she stood and shoved some books aside as if looking for something. "Did you need something, Professor Stephens?"

"No, but I thought you might."

"What is that supposed to mean?"

"That I assumed you were standing outside my classroom for a reason."

Her eyes rounded, and she pressed her lips together. He'd seen her somehow. So, his defense of her had been for her benefit. Why did it matter? It didn't. She'd just determined that. His standoffishness from the moment they met had indicated his attitude toward her, anyway.

An unfamiliar tightness in her chest caused her to lift her chin. "I wanted to catch you before you left and had no idea you would be talking with someone. Perhaps you should have closed the door."

He raised an eyebrow. "I don't close doors when talking with my students, especially female students."

"Well, you could have asked a female professor." She forced a smile. "Not me, of course. No respect there."

He pushed off the doorframe and took a step inside. "It's part of the ritual. No respect until you earn it, and I'm sure you will after you've been here a few more weeks. About the other - I was asked by a female student to address the issue with Stephanie when no other professors would – male or female."

"Nobody else would? That's ridiculous. If there's a dress code, enforce it or drop it."

"Says the lawyer."

So, that was the problem. They'd better clear the air then. Alexis placed her hands flat on the desk and leaned forward. "Do you have something against lawyers?"

"No."

"No? Since the moment we met, you've exhibited a negative attitude toward me. I get the fact that not everyone wants pre-law classes at a Bible college, but you're going to have to live with it."

"Look, I never—"

She raised her hands, palms up. "Live. With. It."

His head drew back, and his mouth thinned, the amusement gone.

She dropped her hands. The three words had carried more antagonism than she'd wanted. What was wrong with her?

She forced her voice to an even tone. "Look, I heard you teaching on the laws of God last week. If you have respect for them, you should have respect for the laws of this country, too."

Luke took a step forward, flattened his hands on her desk as she had and leaned into her space. "You have a chip on your shoulder. I don't know where it came from, but you need to get rid of it. And you have no idea what you're talking about. The laws of God are why I *do* respect the laws of this country. You don't have a monopoly on that."

She straightened and stared into eyes that had changed from green to gray. Beautiful eyes. Long lashes. She opened her mouth to say something but stopped. *What had he just said?* "Okay. I'll give you that, but I'm not the only one with a chip on their shoulder. You want to tell me why you don't want me teaching here?"

"I don't have anything against you teaching here."

"Oh? Your actions at the time we met left me with the distinct impression that you did. And that impression hasn't changed."

"Look, you…" He stopped, stared at her for a moment then stepped back. "I think this …discussion…has gone far enough. If you have something you want to talk to me about, come by tomorrow." He turned.

"No, I…Wait." Alexis put out her hand, but he was at the door. "Please, I…"

He swiveled back, brows lowered, and shot one word at her. "What?"

She cleared her throat. "Jessica's not here today. I'm worried about that, and…"

"Call her."

"I can't."

"Why?"

"I don't have her number."

"Didn't you get it Friday?"

"No, I gave her mine, but didn't get hers."

His look raked the ceiling before he jerked his phone from the case on his belt. He punched the phone a few times and listened. Alexis watched in silence. He frowned, punched the screen a few more times and began to text.

"She'll get back to me. I'll tell her to call you." He slipped the phone into its holder.

"If she can."

"She talked about staying the weekend with a friend. She should be fine."

"*If* she did, and *if* she didn't let her mom or her mom's boyfriend know she'd talked with anyone. *If* she didn't let them know she's pregnant. All *ifs*."

"She's smart enough not to do that."

"I've dealt with lots of women who should have acted smarter than they did. And why isn't she here today? Missing my class is one thing. It's the earliest, but she wasn't in yours either."

"She could be sick."

"Yes, morning sickness."

His glower might scare his students but didn't move Alexis. "You brought her to me. Now you want me to ignore something like this?"

He said nothing for a moment, and the scowl didn't change. "All right then. Grab your bag, your purse. Come on."

"What? Where?"

"If I'm going to her place, you're going with me. You know the legal ramifications around this, I don't."

"Well, I…"

"Are you worried or not?"

She studied him a minute. *Was she? Yes, she was.* "I don't know her well enough to say if this is out of character. Does she skip classes on a whim?"

"She's a regular student; misses sometimes. Not often."

Alexis grabbed her purse and left the other stuff. "We'll take my car."

He stepped into the hall. "I'm not riding in that tuna can."

She twirled the lock on her door. *He was insulting her Jag?* "We're going in my car."

Luke headed back to his classroom. Alexis followed and watched as he gathered up his books and papers and stuffed them into a backpack. "We're going in my truck. If you're so worried about Jessica, you won't have a problem with that. I know where she lives."

"You..." The word huffed through clenched teeth and dropped off. Worry had surrounded her since Jessica had not shown at her first class, but it had taken their discussion and the adrenalin hit from her anger to push her into doing something. Luke knew where the girl lived, and Jessica had come to him with her problem.

She should be thankful that he saw the need. But was there something here she needed to know? She looked across at him. "You have her number on your phone, and you know where she lives. Why?"

"Drove the bus when we took the students to a concert last year. I put all the students' numbers into my phone at the time. Later, I dropped her off because she had no car and no one to pick her up."

"Oh."

"Meet with your approval?"

"It was just a question."

"Your questions sound like an inquisition."

People had told her that before – inside and outside the courtroom. They reached the parking lot, and he headed for his truck. Alexis kept in step. He unlocked his door and climbed in and hit the button that unlocked her side.

He wasn't opening her door for her. Not quite the southern gentleman she'd assumed or was it because he was irritated?

Alexis opened the passenger door and slipped into the seat. She glanced his way while tugging the seatbelt into position. "Look, I didn't mean to sound accusatory. It was just a question."

One for which she'd wanted the answer, though. His relationship to the girl could prove problematic. But she'd keep that to herself.

❧

Neither spoke as he drove. Luke told himself to cool off. Dealing with the woman took more patience than most. Dealing with the girl, Stephanie, hadn't ruffled an iota of his emotions. Compare that to what he was feeling now.

And what was he doing, anyway? All students skipped class from time to time. He'd never gone chasing after any of them. Still, if the girl hadn't stayed at her friend's house this weekend, and if Alexis' instincts were correct...

He shot her a sideways glance. She sat with both her arms and legs crossed. He couldn't help but notice the long legs showing beneath her skirt's modest length. The woman's attractiveness showed even in the business suit – maybe because of it. He wondered if she even knew. Stephanie's words sounded like spite or jealousy.

Luke forced his eyes back to the road. He sensed a depth in Alexis that outweighed her looks. Her obvious concern and defense for abused women – as he had learned at the faculty meeting – was part of that. She didn't stand on the sidelines; she had the courage and fortitude to wade into the battle.

He cleared his throat. "Do you want to do this alone or should we both go to the door when we get there?" Her head turned, and he could feel the heat from her gaze. Her frustration with him hadn't died yet either. *Funny how she'd noticed his wary attitude from the first.*

"We'll both go. Two of the faculty from the college. I think that will add some weight. Remember, I'm not a lawyer here, and I don't want the mother or the boyfriend to know anything but that we're from the college."

"Makes sense. But what reason do we give for showing up at her door?"

"We had an appointment, and she didn't show and didn't

answer her phone. We're just checking on her. That's true. Sort of. The appointment was for class. We won't mention that."

"You've done this before?"

"Checking up on victims in these cases? Oh, yeah."

He turned into the mobile home lot a few minutes later. Not an upscale lot but most of the homes and small yards were well kept. He drove to the back, made a left turn and parked in front of a white mobile home with blue trim. The driveway and carport were empty, but an older Ford Focus with faded turquoise paint sat half in the street and half in the yard.

She beat him out of the truck and to the door, knocking hard. He stepped close behind her. Nothing moved or stirred. She knocked again, louder. He grimaced; the woman wasn't shy.

"Jessica?" Alexis' voice rose to match her knocking. "Jessica, are you in there?"

Luke glanced back toward a screen door that Alexis had passed when she shot up the driveway. He thought he saw movement and took a step back.

"Jessica, are you all right?" Alexis' voice came from behind him as he walked toward the screen door.

"Hey." His own voice rose over hers. "Hey, you, in the screen porch. We're looking for Jessica Saltare. Have you seen her?" No one moved or answered. Alexis' voice had stopped, and she moved his way.

"You think we should call the police?" she asked, her voice raised.

Luke turned his head. Was she serious or calling a bluff?

The screen door opened, and a man edged his body into the doorway. He glared at them through narrowed, red-rimmed eyes. "What do you want?"

His unkempt hair and dirty t-shirt didn't give Luke a good feeling. He stared at a spot on the man's shirt. *Was that blood?*

Alexis pushed in front of him. "We're looking for Jessica. She missed an appointment this morning, and that's not like her. She's not answering her phone or her messages, and she's always prompt doing that."

"Who are you?"

Alexis introduced them before Luke had time to respond. The woman meant business, that was for sure.

"Do you know where she is?" Alexis asked.

"No. She ain't here." A skeletal hand started to close the door.

Luke grabbed the handle. "Just a minute."

"I ain't got a minute." The man tugged at the door.

A pungent odor circled the man and almost caused Luke to step back. "Who are you? I thought just Jessica and her mom lived here."

"I'm a friend."

"Well, where's her mom then?"

"At work."

"Does she know Jessica's missing?"

"Jessica ain't missing."

"Then where is she?"

"None of your business." The man yanked on the door. When Luke yanked back, the other man straightened. "You lookin' for a fight?"

Luke raised an eyebrow. Their heights were about even, but he had twenty-five to thirty pounds on the man.

Alexis stepped closer. "We just want to find Jessica."

"I told you, she ain't here. Now—"

Something crashed inside the mobile home.

Luke's head shot around. He stepped backward, looking at the other door. "What was that?"

"Nothing!"

The screen door ripped from Luke's hand. Alexis grabbed it and tried to force it open again. The click of the lock met her efforts.

"Let us in, or we're calling the police." Her voice rose as

the man hurried away from them and into the house. "We're not leaving. I'm dialing 911 right now."

She had her phone out but didn't move. Luke watched her. Something was up with the man, but what? They could be wrong in their suspicions.

"What are you doing?" he asked.

"Waiting. I want to see what he does. Someone or something else is in there."

Luke nodded. "I can use my pocket knife and cut the screen door to get in."

Alexis raised her head, eyes widening, and seemed to consider it for a moment. "No, not yet." Both stopped as some other noise came from inside. "Was that a scream? Muffled?"

"Or cut off. Call 911." He yanked the knife from his pocket. Its two and a half inch blade would do what was needed.

The door at the side banged open and the scruffy-haired man ran out. He held a backpack in one hand like a weapon and ran straight for them. Luke stepped out to meet him. The man's eyes flicked to the blade in Luke's hand, and he swerved and headed for the car.

"Hey!" Luke yelled.

Alexis grabbed his arm. "Let him go, Luke. He could have a gun with him or one in the car."

His muscles tightened, and Alexis' fingers sunk into his arm.

"No. Jessica is more important."

Luke hesitated. It had been six years since he'd faced combat – six years that dissolved like they were yesterday. Adrenalin surged through him.

The car door slammed. The engine started. The Ford swerved their way, and they both jumped backward.

Luke grabbed for the carport's support pole and righted himself. The car squealed into a U-turn and accelerated down the street.

Alexis' voice came from behind him. He glanced around just as she ran for the trailer's open door. He straightened and limped after her.

As he stepped inside, he folded the knife and slipped it into his pocket. The trailer had a mixture of smells. None good, but one he knew he could identify.

"Jessica!" Alexis yelled. "Jessica!"

From the end of the hallway came a muffled cry. A bureau covered a bedroom door. Next to it an ottoman lay on its side.

Alexis grabbed the bureau, but Luke shoved her aside. He put a hand on each side, rocked it back and forth and shimmied it out of the way.

Before he'd cleared the doorway, Alexis pushed past him into the room. Her voice rose with the girl's name then dropped into what sounded like a curse. He moved around the bureau, but Alexis stepped in front of him.

"Wait outside." Her voice roughened with command.

His one glimpse had given him more information than he needed. He whirled, grabbed his phone, and punched 911. The man had left the girl naked, bruised and bloodied. His hands shook as he waited for the operator.

Chapter 7

By the time they arrived back at the college, night had saturated the ground with dew, and the moon had risen then dropped in the sky. Alexis put her head back against the truck's seat. Exhaustion traveled through every nerve and muscle in her body, and her head ached.

Luke stopped the truck next to her car, the only one in the staff parking lot. The electric poles scattered yellow light into Luke's truck and across her Jaguar. Alexis didn't move, not because she didn't want to, but because she had to wait for her legs and arms to respond to her mental "Get out."

In the semi-darkness, he turned her way. "So, this is your world."

Hearing the harshness in his tone and not sure of his meaning, she said nothing.

"You have my sympathy – and admiration." His tone softened. "Your world is not pretty."

She rolled her head back and forth. "Cops and robbers, only mine are victims and abusers. Yes. It's what I do – or did until a few months ago."

"Why?"

"I hate the violence perpetrated against women and children."

His silence indicated he thought she had more to say, but she remained quiet. Pain formed a dark remembrance in the corner of her mind. He'd asked earlier if she had chased down other victims whose cases she was working. She'd answered yes; perhaps now he saw the reason why.

Luke shifted his hands on the steering wheel. "'Vengeance

is mine,' says the Lord; but I would gladly wreak vengeance on the man who did this."

"Then you know how I feel."

"Yes, but you get to."

"Sometimes." She knew the frustration, the anger of not being able to help. When he hit the steering wheel, it didn't surprise her.

"How do you cope with that?"

"What? Not winning a case?"

"Yes."

"Not well."

The silence stretched again before he added, "Jessica was glad you were there – when the police arrived, and in the ambulance, and again at the hospital."

"I wanted to be there. The assault is only heightened by the investigative procedures."

"I'm beginning to understand that. At least the first officer on the scene seemed professional and caring."

"Yes, and he called in female backup. And talked to her about the Order of Protection against Leland, if they find him. Whether they will, I don't know. Her mom didn't know too many of his friends or even where his family lives." She shifted in the seat. "That detective was a different story."

"I noticed."

In the dark cab, she couldn't see his face, but the tautness of his voice made her own frustration ease.

She'd wanted to slap the man. Hard. "Men like that, who act like the victim caused the rape, do more than almost anything else to keep victims from reporting. It's hard enough to be violated like that without fending off sneers and questions that tear at who you are. If Jessica hadn't asked me to stay during the questioning – plus the fact that both you and I could give evidence to her claim – his attitude and questions might have humiliated her more."

Surprisingly, Jessica had answered his questions with poise and dignity. She'd kept a rein on her emotions until the man left. Alexis had reached out as the door closed and enfolded Jessica in her arms and let her cry.

"Tell me more about the rape test kit."

"What?" She drew her mind back. "Oh, the kit is used to collect forensic or physical evidence from the victim – an *hours-long* examination, as you just discovered. They collect hair and fibers from clothing and the victim. Also, body fluids such as saliva and semen. All of it can help in identifying the rapist. You can imagine what kind of exam they do to collect those. It's horrible to be raped, then questioned by law enforcement, and finally to have to go through such a physical and emotional ordeal at the hospital." She stared out the window. "It's no wonder the vast majority of rapes go unreported."

"You stuck by her the whole time and had them call the rape crisis counselors. Jessica and her mother have a lot to thank you for."

She waved her hand, dismissing his comment. "Jessica will need the counseling now and in the months to come. I hope she takes advantage of it."

"If you were licensed to practice here, would you take Jessica's case?"

She hesitated. Wasn't that her whole reason for leaving Atlanta? Leaving her job? To put this all behind her? She'd come here looking for a new life, not more of the same.

"I can't practice here. That's the reality."

He said nothing, and she looked away.

"Where do we go from here?"

"To see that scumbag put away?"

"Yes."

She rolled her shoulders forward, rolled her head side to side again. How could she run from this? Running from herself was one thing, running when it involved someone else was another.

"I'll do whatever I can."

"I knew you would. Jessica will need you. She'll need

someone who knows the ins and outs of this."

"What I know is this – and since you're a man this is a prickly subject – but men are scumbags. I admit to meeting a few good ones, but by and large..."

"By and large what you see are scumbags."

"Yes."

"Well, if what you see and hear is what we saw today, I understand your sentiments."

"Thank you."

After a moment, he said, "After what Jessica told us about her mom, Dawn surprised me."

"Encouraging Jessica to make the complaint?"

"Yes."

"A mother bear acting to an attack on her cub. Let's see if she stays with that after the first of her anger disappears."

"You think she could change her mind?" His voice ratcheted up a notch.

"It's happens. Other moms have changed their minds. Victims have, too. Dawn kicked Leland out Friday night when Jessica told her she was pregnant, and I'm sure neither of them expected him to show back up again. If the girl had gone to her friend's instead of feeling like she had to tell her mother right away..." Regret filled her heart, and Alexis folded her hands in her lap. "If I had gone over there after my first class..."

"I wondered if you were going there. Don't. You have nothing to feel guilty about. You know who the perpetrator is here. Keep your eyes on him. The man knew their routine, when she'd be home alone."

"My guess is he watched from down the street and waited to see when Jessica's mom left."

"I wonder why he hung around from morning until evening. You'd think..." He stopped.

Alexis knew he didn't want to put words to the thoughts in his mind. She'd wanted the same many times.

"I think he was waiting for Dawn to come back from

work." She cleared her throat. "He wanted revenge on them both."

"Just for throwing him out?"

"For that and all that it meant." Alexis tightened her voice. "I'm sure he has a sexual relationship with Dawn – and a free place to stay. Add to that food and probably money Dawn gave him. He's most likely tried to get Dawn on drugs."

"The place smelled like weed – like marijuana."

She nodded. "Since it's legal in more and more states, most people are dropping their wariness of it. A shame, especially since it can be laced with other things. He's probably her supplier if she's using and that is another hook he has in her."

She threw open the door and climbed down, standing for a moment, staring at the ground. Taking a deep breath of cold air, she raised her head. Beyond her, dawn showed in the silvered outline of the dark mountains.

"Alexis?"

She glanced into the lit cab. "Yeah?"

"Are you okay?"

"What?"

"Are you okay?" He lifted one side of his mouth. "I can't do anything about the fact that I'm a man, but I've been told that I'm a good listener."

"No." She said it quick. He was a man. She appreciated all he'd said and done today, but could she talk with him about her feelings? No.

She opened the car's door, leaned over, and set her purse on the passenger seat. "Thank you for the offer, though. I...I do appreciate it." She slid into the seat, making sure he knew she wouldn't change her mind.

"Okay. What's your number?"

"What?"

"Your phone number. I'll plug it into my phone, call you, and you'll have mine. If something else comes up, give me a call. I'd like to be kept in the loop, if possible."

"Oh, I..." She hesitated. *Come on. Just give it to him.* When she told him, he punched it in and a few seconds later, she heard her phone give its lilting ring.

Okay, he had it; and she had his. Not that she'd use it. "Thanks."

Luke nodded and started the truck's engine. "See you in a few hours."

She clipped the seatbelt, pushed the start button, and flipped on the lights. A few hours? Ah, work. She watched as his truck headed for the exit.

With her hand on the wheel, she hesitated. *What would it feel like to trust again?*

Her boss in Atlanta, Tim Bradley, had earned it if anyone had, but even in five years, she'd only let her guard down twice. Both times had to do with cases she should have won, wanted with all her heart to win, but had lost because the victims wouldn't testify. Fear and humiliation had won instead, and the last victim, Jennifer Johnson, had died later at the hand of her abuser. When she got the news, Alexis could not contain her anger nor her tears.

Tim had talked with and comforted her like the fatherly, family man he was. But Tim also knew the courts, the victims, and the perpetrators. And he knew justice and Alexis' thirst for it. He'd comforted and encouraged and talked her into forging on. Losses came, but so did wins – and this abuser was now a murderer. They both wanted to see justice done, and they'd done it. That particular perpetrator now awaited sentencing. She'd given her notice as soon as the guilty verdict was returned.

She moved her head back against the Jaguar's seat, inhaling the leather scent, pressing her shoulders into its coolness. Exhaustion eased up from her stomach into her arms and shoulders. She put the car into drive and crossed the parking lot. Her heart gave a quick jolt when Luke's truck lights came on near the exit.

He'd waited for her.

੭

The early light of morning sifted between the tree's remaining leaves and painted the living room floor. Luke's pacing stopped. He swung to face the window and stared past the huge tree to the mountains beyond. He inhaled, filled his lungs, and held it for a second or two before exhaling, and pulled control from the depths of his soul.

The animals needed tending, and there was work to do before he left for class. He'd get no sleep, but he couldn't force himself back out the door, yet.

Focusing on the mountains stirred questions he'd faced before. God had made them. No matter when he looked out, they were always there. Steady, strong, immoveable.

He rubbed a hand down his face. The picture of Jessica on the stretcher as they wheeled her to the ambulance crowded his mind. Her bruised face, the matted hair. Alexis had found a bathrobe for her, shielding her from the curious eyes of the neighbors. She'd sent him a long look before climbing into the ambulance with the girl.

Lord, you made the mountains, couldn't you do a better job with humanity?

He whirled from the window, grabbing the water bottle he'd set on the end table. It crushed in his hand. Water squirted and flooded his fingers, running onto the floor.

Scripture coursed through his mind. *I have set before you life and death, blessings and curses. Now choose life, so that you and your children may live.*

The gift of choice. He set the water bottle back on the table and closed his eyes. They'd played out this scenario once before – he and God – six years ago. People chose which way they wanted to go. They chose God or not. He'd had no problem choosing to fight what he saw as evil. But what would he choose after a bomb exploded killing and maiming those he cared for?

He'd chosen God again, chosen to believe that the God he served was good and worthy to be praised even when he could not understand why things happened as they did.

After that decision, God had led him here, to Appalachian Christian College. Whoever thought the warrior would find such satisfaction in teaching, in directing lives? God had given him a place of influence with these young adults, and he respected that, prized it even.

But tonight something different had touched his life.

You aren't going to show me this just to let me sit and do nothing about it, are you? You've called Alexis. I see that, even if she's run from the calling right now. You haven't let her get away. He ran a hand down his face again, directed his focus to the mountains again.

She's fragile, isn't she? Under that gruff self-sufficiency is something young and vulnerable. Help her, Lord. Protect her. Help Jessica, too. Bring her comfort tonight and in the days to come. And show me what you want me to do.

≈

Alexis grabbed a piece of chocolate from the desk drawer beside her and popped the whole thing into her mouth before eyeing the stack of essays again.

Luke had hung close at the hospital last night. His concern for Jessica impressed her. He had her brother's capacity for care. She smiled, and perhaps, his capacity for anger. Anger could be a good thing. When Luke snapped at an inappropriate question the investigating detective asked, the detective knew he had both of them watching out for Jessica. Alexis had appreciated Luke's support. And he'd waited for her to leave last night. More protection.

The pile of essays blurred, and her mind returned to an idea stirring inside her. Both she and Dawn feared that Leland might return. They needed a safe house, but no beds were available. Alexis had checked, and since she wouldn't be the attorney on this case, she could offer a place to stay. She'd wanted to do that in the past and couldn't, but now? Would it work? Would they accept her offer?

She glanced at her watch. Jessica would be released from the hospital sometime around 7:00 PM. Just under the twenty-four-hour mark for the hospital and the insurance. In less than two hours, she needed to make a decision.

A movement startled her, and she raised her head.

Luke stood just inside the door. "How're you holding up?"

"I'm fine."

"Would you tell me if you weren't?" He held up a hand before she could say anything. "No need to answer. I'll change the subject. How's Jessica?"

"Her mom answered when I called. Jessica is doing well according to her. They'll be getting out soon."

His lower lip moved as if he wanted to say something, but he only nodded. "They're having a concert before the game tonight. You going?"

Alexis blinked, trying to hopscotch her mind to the new topic. She looked at the books and papers scattered across her desk. "I have too much to do. Grading is harder than teaching and takes longer."

Luke pushed away from the door. "Exactly why you need a break. Especially after yesterday."

"And what about you?"

"Same as you. After trying to grade the essays I assigned, I wished I'd never assigned them." He glanced at her desk. "Even if I do all mine online. I decided I needed a break. Come on. It starts in a few minutes. I heard they have pizza and hotdogs."

"Oh, yummy."

He smiled, his eyes warming; and her stomach did a strange little flip.

"If you're as tired as you looked a moment ago, you're making bad judgments on those papers, anyway."

Bad judgments? On the papers or other things? Was she dragging her feet about Jessica because of her tiredness? She took a deep breath, looked down at the papers again and shoved back her chair. "I have a quick call to make, and then

I'll come." She lifted her arm, focused on her watch. "For an hour."

"Not staying for the game?"

"Picking up Jessica and her mom."

His brows lifted, but he nodded. "Want me to ride shotgun?"

She lifted her own brow. "I think we'll be okay, but you mean you'd ride in the Jag?"

"If I had to."

She grinned, and he grinned back. Her stomach did the little flip thing again, and she turned her back to him, shielding herself from that smile.

"Let me call them." Grabbing the phone, she punched in Dawn's number. After talking with her for a couple minutes, she received their acceptance of her offer until something opened up in a safe house.

"You're having them stay at your place?"

She turned to find his eyes showing concern. "Yes."

"Is that dangerous?"

She shrugged. "Not really. No one's supposed to know where they are."

"No one's *supposed* to."

Alexis ignored the tone and pulled her purse from the bottom desk drawer, shoving her phone inside. "I know how to protect myself. This isn't my first case."

He gave a mocking bow. "Of course. Sorry. Why don't you leave your purse here? You won't need it at the concert."

"I always bring my purse."

"Like my mom."

She straightened and tilted her head. He'd used that tone when talking about her coffee, too. A tone filled with long suffering and patience.

Her hands went to her hips. "Do you mind not comparing me to your mom?"

He chuckled. "I like my mom, but the comparison ends with coffee and purses. Trust me."

That phrase again. *Trust me.*

His chuckle, though, sent a third wave of warmth through her. He took her arm and eased her toward the door. What was happening? She couldn't think past his hand on her arm. Indecision raced through her. Pull her arm away or leave it? A moment later, he dropped his hand, and she battled both relief and regret.

The gym echoed with youthful voices. They slipped between students and other faculty members, and Alexis nodded at the ones she knew. Luke led the way to the far end, where a number of students moved around a portable stage. They stopped a few feet away, and he nodded to a few of the musicians.

A young man with a blonde ponytail adjusted his glasses and ran his hand over the keys on his keyboard. "We've got a new song, Professor Stephens. Want to hear it?"

"Sure."

"Probably need to practice some first." The man flipped his head around, bouncing his ponytail. "Jaleel, you with me?"

A tall young man, his skin dark and glistening in the gym lights, slung his guitar strap over his head. "Give me a minute." He began to tune the guitar.

Another student that she recognized from her class slipped behind the drums and lifted the sticks. He winked at her and began to spin the sticks.

Luke chuckled again. "You've got an admirer."

She shot him a frown. "I don't think I'd go that far."

"I don't know. I make bet you had a few additions the first week of class."

"What does that mean?"

His eyes held amusement. "That our male students know a good thing when they see it." The drums started, the keyboard joined in; and he said nothing more.

Two female students stepped up to the open mics, and the young man at the keyboard began to sing.

"Jesus, hope of the world, I stand amazed…"

Students began to gather behind her and Luke. The talking quieted. Alexis glanced around. Most of the students and faculty were focused on the singers. Luke sang softly. Something moved across the gym - like a wave.

Alexis shifted uneasily. She hugged herself and wondered how she could slip out. The crowd tightened and grew. Some began to sing as Luke was doing with the group on stage. The lights dimmed. No one seemed to take notice, so she focused on the musicians.

So serious. It really is worship. They worship this Jesus.

When the song ended, everyone clapped, some hooted. Luke gave a sharp whistle, and she jumped.

He grinned down at her. "They're good."

She nodded. She could agree with that. For non-professionals, the sound had surpassed what she assumed she'd hear.

"Hey, sing that song you guys were practicing this afternoon," a voice shouted.

"Which one, Darryl?"

"Yeah, dude." Mr. Ponytail said. "We practiced them all."

"Just start the program, will you?" Another person yelled. "We got a game tonight."

The next song talked about the struggles the singer had in his life, comparing his life to a prison, and how Jesus had set him free.

They looked like many groups she'd seen. The lead singer at the mic had hair that flung back and forth as his head swung from side to side, his guitar-playing and small jumps back from the microphone echoed many other musicians, but the look on his face differed.

Alexis concentrated on the words, trying to make sense of them. Why did the singer think he was unworthy, and what was it about Jesus that made him feel redeemed and free? What was he saying about a new life and new name?

New life.

Again.

The singer was talking about shaking off chains, and that was what Alexis wanted to do – shake off the constant reminders of what had happened in the past. She swallowed. Something about it stirred feelings she could not identify.

What she really needed was to get out of here, get away from this music. As the song ended, she touched Luke. He bent his head her way.

"I'm going to slip out and head to the hospital."

"Already?"

"They could release Jessica early."

He studied her a moment, and she forced herself not to move.

"Okay. I'll walk you to your car."

"No." She caught her inflection and cleared her throat. "No. That's not necessary. I'm fine. Besides, you're enjoying the music."

"Yes." He studied her a minute. "You're okay?"

"Yes. I think it would be better to go now rather than later."

"This is a great thing you're doing, letting Jessica and her mom stay with you."

His words made her uncomfortable. She wasn't doing that much – had never been able to do as much as she wanted.

"Not really. They need a place. I'm just providing a place until something opens up for them." She glanced at all the students crowding around. The band started to play again, and she leaned in close. "We need to keep this between us. It's a safe house."

He nodded. "Yes. Sorry. I'll remember that."

She waved and slipped away, excusing herself to get through the crowd. The song filled the room again. Something about amazing grace, but not the *Amazing Grace* she'd heard during her life. This was different, more modern, upbeat. She stopped before going out the door and turned to look back.

The students and faculty swayed with the beat, some with hands in the air, some moving their heads, all concentrating on the music.

Amazing grace, unfailing love... The air seemed to shimmy, to become heavy all around her. Tears filled her eyes. She needed to get out of here, get free of whatever was happening.

She shoved open the door, ran past some students who stood talking outside, and made straight for her car.

The familiar seats and leather smell soothed her. She inhaled, taking comfort in the car's scent. Shoving her hand into the glove compartment, she grabbed a bar of chocolate.

The songs bothered her.

But why run? If there were no God, no Jesus who died on a cross and rose from the dead as her brother would have her believe, then why run? Why were they so enraptured by this...man? Another man; one her brother said she could trust.

She pulled the paper from the candy and turned on her radio. Find some other songs.

Alexis wheeled out of the parking lot, heading into town. She finished the chocolate and hit the radio again. She'd taken her own music out awhile ago, but hadn't put it back which left her at the mercy of the radio stations. Nothing good. She grabbed her phone and called Jessica to let her know she was on the way.

As she dropped her phone on the seat, a car veered in front of her. Red tail lights blazed. She slammed on the brakes. Tires screeching, the Jag vaulted to a stop. A man leapt from the car in front of her and sprinted back, pounding her windshield. She couldn't see his face, hadn't glimpsed it as he ran. All she could see was his chest.

"Open the window!"

She edged the window down an inch. "What are you—"

Cursing flowed over her, and the man bent down. Leland's hard eyes bored into hers. "Stay away from Jessica, do you

hear? If you know what's good for you, you'll keep away."
He cursed again and slammed his fist against the Jag's top.
"You hear me? You'll get more than her if you don't."

Alexis groped for her purse, grabbed it from the adjacent
seat, and snatched the zipper down. A moment later, she held
her pistol in her hand. "Get away from the car!"

The man jumped back, eyes widening. "Hey. Don't get so
upset."

She made a motion with the gun. "Back up farther."

As Leland edged away, she started to climb from the Jag
but hesitated. The man might jump her. Where was her
phone? She gave a quick glance at the seat next to her. On
the floor? She heard movement and whipped her head
around. Leland ran for his Ford Focus and yanked the door
open.

"Hey!" She yelled. "Hey!"

The other car surged forward. She scrambled to find her
phone and yanked it out from under the seat. Glancing up,
she saw the Ford disappear down the road. She laid her head
against the steering wheel. No one had passed them. The
whole incident probably took forty-five seconds. If that. She
shook herself. She'd pulled her .380 semi-automatic more
than once for protection, but her heart had never slapped her
chest as hard as it did now.

She put her gun back in its compartment of her concealed
carry purse. Leland was gone, but after she picked up Jessica
and Dawn, she'd call the police.

Her hand froze on the shift. How had Leland known where
to find her?

She sighed. She and Luke told him they were from the
college. He'd obviously been waiting for her and followed
her from the college. Well, she'd make sure that didn't
happen again.

Chapter 8

Luke's attention was drawn from the mountains outside his second-story office window to the man climbing from a black truck in the parking lot. Not one of the students or faculty or anyone he knew. Tall and thin and about his own age, the man circled the back of the truck and crossed the parking lot before heading up the front walkway.

The man stopped...dead.

The words were a cliché, but the man's actions gave evidence to why someone had coined the phrase – the man froze.

Following the other's gaze, he saw Alexis coming down the administration building's sidewalk. Her head down, she was stuffing papers into the large handbag she carried. Finished, she raised her head. The stopped dead rhetoric worked for her, too, but only for a moment. The next instant, she dropped everything she held and raced down the sidewalk. The man took a step forward just as she flung herself into his arms. He stumbled with the force of her impact.

One side of Luke's mouth lifted even as something hard stabbed into his chest. If she'd thrown herself at him like that, they'd both be on the ground. Instead, the other man recovered, swung her in a circle then set her down and wrapped his arms around her. They stood holding each other for a long time.

Luke stepped away from the window. Whatever the reunion was, it wasn't his to watch. But something drew him back. He took a deep breath and glanced out again.

They broke the embrace. Alexis stepped away and raised her hands in a familiar gesture. Luke's smile widened. Whoever the man was, she was telling him off – but good. The stranger stood and took it until she finished. Luke agreed with the inaction. No sense trying to defend yourself against that tornado.

When she slowed and dropped her hands, the man enfolded her in his arms again.

This time, Luke made a definite turn from the window. He didn't need the squeeze in his chest to tell him what he'd been denying for the last couple of days. The woman wasn't just special to God. She'd wormed her way inside him, too.

He took a deep breath and headed out. Maybe he'd get to meet this paragon of her affection, because he had no doubt this man was just that. She wasn't the kind to throw herself at too many men.

It only took a minute to get from his office, down the stairs and out the door. The man was holding Alexis by her shoulders and nodding.

"You know, I would have been here if possible." The words carried. Emotion laced them, but Luke couldn't place it. Sadness? Regret? Guilt?

Alexis' response was too low for his hearing.

A smile lit the other man's face. "He's doing fine. He's a miracle."

"But I wanted to see him – both Sharee and the baby. Why didn't you bring them?" Alexis voice reached his ears as he neared them.

"I thought you wanted me home," the tall man said. "You mean you wanted them, too?"

"Don't start with me—"

"What baby?" Luke interjected over her shoulder.

Alexis jerked her head around. The other man straightened and sent him a questioning look.

"I did hear 'baby,' didn't I?" Luke asked. If he had to force the introduction, he would. Better to know now if he read this relationship right or not. He'd make sure he kept his feelings to himself if he had. Not that they'd made themselves known to him until a few minutes ago.

"Yes." Alexis' voice sounded impatient but touched with amusement. "You heard baby. John and Sharee's baby." Alexis nodded his way. "Luke, this is my brother, John. John, Luke Stephens."

"Brother?" Luke worked hard to keep the surprise from his voice.

"Yeah." Brown eyes the same color as Alexis' scrutinized him.

Something tight loosened inside Luke's chest. He smiled and extended his hand. The other man's handshake was firm.

"Luke?" the man repeated. "Good to meet you. Do you teach here like Alexis?"

Luke couldn't stop the feeling of relief sweeping through him nor the twist of amusement to his mouth. "Not like Alexis. From what the students say, she has a style all her own. But yes, I teach."

Alexis whirled on him. "What does that mean?"

He held up a hand. "Nothing, Dar—" He coughed. "Nothing. Just a statement."

Luke didn't miss the narrowing of her brother's eyes and the speculative look he threw him. Darling? Is that what he'd started to say? Better be on his way before he messed up big time.

Alexis frowned and surveyed him.

He gave his best smile. "Your brother? From around here?"

"No, John and his family just arrived from Indonesia."

Luke lifted a brow. "That's quite a plane trip."

"It was." Her brother's eyes shifted from him to Alexis. "But coming home is well worth it."

Luke nodded. *Close family.*

"I don't mean to be rude," John said, "but Sharee and the baby are waiting at the cabin for us. We're trying to get out to dinner between feedings."

Luke laughed. "I understand that. Don't let me keep you. I have some feeding up to do myself. Nice to meet you." He nodded at John then at Alexis. "See you Monday."

He walked past them and to the parking lot, his face breaking into a grin. *Brother. Thank you, Lord.*

He stopped with his fingers on the door handle. Had his brain shut down? She's not whom you're looking for. You know that. Too serious and too pretty. Don't ask for trouble.

"I don't care what he said, Mom. He's a liar, and you know it."

Jessica's voice reached Alexis as she thrust open the door of the condo a few minutes later. She wanted to change clothes before John and Sharee picked her up. From now on, she planned to have a change of clothes at the college. She stepped into the foyer and paused with her hand on the knob.

"You listen to me, girl. If I say—" Dawn's voice stopped when Jessica put a finger to her mouth. Both stood just inside the kitchen. Dawn turned and looked Alexis' way.

Alexis pushed the door closed. "Hi. Am I interrupting?"

"No." Jessica came forward and lifted the extra books Alexis carried. "Let me get these. We were discussing what we could make for dinner."

"Can you put them on the bookshelf? Thanks. I'm running back out to meet my brother and his wife for dinner. They're in town for a couple of weeks. So don't worry about me."

She headed for her bedroom. What had cropped up that Jessica didn't want to share? Dumping her purse and briefcase on the bed, she yanked the clip from her hair, pulled her jeans and a sweater from the closet and slipped into the bathroom. In a few minutes, she walked back down the hall, over the wooden floor, and dropped into a barrel accent chair.

Across the Chinese area rug, Jessica and Dawn sat at

opposite ends of the sofa. Jessica played with one of the sofa's accent pillows.

Before John and Sharee picked her up, perhaps she'd have a few minutes to figure out what that first sentence meant. Who was a liar?

"I'm sorry about running out tonight, but I haven't seen them for a year; and they have a new baby."

"A new baby?" Dawn's eye flicked to Jessica, and Jessica's hand dropped to her stomach. "Where are they from?"

"Indonesia right now."

"Indonesia?"

"Yes, they're missionaries to Indonesia. They work with a human trafficking group there and also help fly supplies into villages where there are no roads."

Jessica pulled her legs under her. "Really? How awesome. I hope I can do something like that when I graduate."

Dawn's head swerved her way, a frown highlighting her face. "Why would you want to do that?"

"Mom! Why do you think? That's why I chose Appalachian. I want to do something worthwhile. Something for God."

"You would just leave me and go to some foreign country like that?" Her mother's voice rose, and she flung her head around toward Alexis. "Is this what that college teaches? I knew it sounded funny when she started talking about attending there last year."

Alexis raised a hand. "Believe me, I felt the same way you did when my brother and his wife flew over there. What did they think they could achieve going half way around the world? But you know..." She smiled. "If I hadn't heard first-hand how they are helping girls caught in sex trafficking – well, I'd still feel the same way. But the group they're with has rescued a number of girls and helped set up a safe place for them, a place where they can learn a trade to support themselves. And if John hadn't told me the stories of flying into the jungles to places where they have no food, no hospitals; how he picks up people seriously ill or hurt and flies them back to the mainland for treatment... If I hadn't heard about it first hand, I would be wondering just like you."

"See, Mom." The girl turned toward Dawn. "I want to do that."

"Well, how would you pay for that? You don't have a husband, and how do you expect to find one in a college with less than seven hundred students?"

Jessica jumped to her feet. "You see what I put up with, Professor Jergenson?"

"I'm just trying to get you to see reality. You're just like Leland said—"

"Wait a minute." Alexis waved a hand and smiled. "Arguing like this won't help anything. I know you're both stressed. A lot has happened lately. How did things go filing the complaint and meeting with the prosecutor?" She had offered to go with them, but Dawn resisted, and Alexis had dropped the matter.

Dawn snorted. "Well, something came up with the prosecutor. We talked with someone else but have to go back again."

"That's too bad. The legal system can be frustrating."

"Can be?" The words jumped. "I want you to know—"

"Mom. It's not Professor Jergenson's fault."

"Call me Alexis, Jessica; and it's okay. I know the system is far from perfect."

"Yeah, well." Dawn lowered her voice. "And I wasn't sure about filing that complaint."

"But you did file it?"

"Yeah, yeah. Jessica insisted."

"I need to ask you something." They must have caught the tone of her voice. Jessica leaned back against the couch. Her mother crossed her arms. "When I came in, you were talking about someone. Was it Leland?"

Dawn slid a sideways look at her daughter. "No."

"No? Well, has he contacted you? Because if you have any idea where he is, we can send the police there. The Order of Protection often takes ten days unless he is arrested and arraigned. The judge can order it right then if he feels it's necessary." Neither Jessica nor Dawn said anything. "I need to know if he knows where you are. You need a safe place, and if he knows you're here, you're no longer safe."

"No." Dawn said again. "We were talking about someone else...about Jessica's father."

Alexis studied her. The woman had no idea how many similar cases Alexis had handled. Leland had called. Certainty of that fact came from a mountain of experience. But what had he said to make Dawn listen to him?

"Is that right, Jessica?"

The girl's eyes flew to her mom. "Yes...I...yes."

"You were talking about your father, not Leland?"

"I...yeah, we were."

"Because if you know where Leland is..."

"No," Dawn crossed her arms over her chest. "Jessica's father heard about the attack. Somehow. So, he called."

Alexis nodded even though her instincts told her Dawn was lying. Later, she'd see if a private talk with Jessica elicited different information.

Her office's mirror captured the reflection. Alexis held the dress to her chest as she'd done the evening before but didn't cry again. Wouldn't.

Even though she, John, Sharee, and the baby had gone out last night, Alexis should have realized they would never let her skip her birthday today. And John told her last night's pizza would never do. They'd take her someplace special, without little Johnnie, so they could dress up. He'd grinned at Sharee. A grown-up dinner, he said; and that's when she realized they needed relief from their own stress as much as she did from hers. They all needed a night out.

Tears had risen after John and Sharee dropped her off last night. Missing her dad and feeling more alone than usual, she'd pulled dresses from her closet, looking for something to wear for her birthday dinner. When she pulled the black, lace dress out, the emotional weight she'd carried all day detonated; and she'd dropped to the floor, sobbing.

Her talk with Jessica would not happen until later.

Now, she slid the black dress over her head. The cool, smoothness of the fabric caressed her skin. Alexis stepped for a second time to her office coat closet and stared at herself in the long mirror. The dress' lining hugged her body while the black lace skimmed over the top of it. Her bare arms and shoulders showed between the lace's intricate pattern.

Turning back to her desk, she picked up the diamond solitaire necklace her mom had given her last Christmas and clipped it around her neck. The matching earrings came next. She unhooked the comb that held her hair and let it drop to her shoulders then brushed it out before slipping on the high heels. Turning, she faced the mirror again.

"A smile, Alexis." Her father had teased the first time she wore the dress, three years earlier. "You're a lovely woman, and you shouldn't try to hide it. Now smile."

Biting the bottom of her lip, she drew a deep breath and closed the closet door. John had promised to pick her up at 7:00, and he would be waiting in the parking lot.

She grabbed the purse she'd picked out for tonight and threw her usual stuff into it. The gun slid into the concealed carry compartment. The number of styles for concealed carry had flummoxed her at first, but later she enjoyed buying different purses for different occasions. She could carry a gun anywhere. And as she'd found more than once, that had a distinct advantage.

Pulling back the curtain from the glass in her office door, she stepped outside and darted down the hall to the steps. Through the large window, she could see the far mountains.

Pink smeared the darkening sky. Her hand on the railing, she glanced toward the parking lot and stopped.

Luke stood with John and Sharee next to John's truck. Her heart thudded. Her mouth went dry, and she tugged at the side of her dress. It hung two inches above her knees, shorter than any skirt she wore for class. She licked her lips. John had seen it before, of course. Ditto with Sharee. Her dad had said she looked stunning in it, so why did she feel so nervous all of a sudden? *So exposed?*

It would be cool outside. Perhaps she should get her coat.

She stared at the parking lot. Sharee laughed and put a hand on John's arm. Her brother slipped an arm around his wife and drew her close. He rested his chin on the top of her head. Alexis smiled. Sharee's petite stature had surprised her when they first met. Alexis, John and her parents all could add *tall* to their resumes. Sharee's five-foot-two had surprised them. But her brother's love for his wife and Sharee's love for him warmed Alexis' heart. That was what marriage was supposed to be.

The shiny blue dress Sharee wore gently clung to her curves. Alexis swallowed. If Sharee felt comfortable then Alexis should, too.

She started down the stairs at a slower pace and made her way to the sidewalk. When she stepped onto the paved lot near the men's trucks, all three of the others looked her way. Sharee and John smiled, but Luke's reaction had her tugging at the skirt of the dress again.

His eyes widened and a moment later his mouth opened, but nothing came out. John leaned over, said something, and laughed. Luke's mouth closed. She stopped beside them.

Sharee threw her arms around her and hugged. "You look beautiful."

Alexis dropped her face into Sharee's shoulder length hair, feeling heat in her face. "Thank you. Sorry I'm late."

"No problem. We had time to talk with Luke." Sharee waved his way.

"I agree with Sharee," John said, hugging her, too. "You look beautiful, and that opinion is shared by all, I'm sure."

"John..." Alexis tried to cut him off.

"Isn't it, Luke?"

Luke's gaze met her brother's then settled on her. "Yes. You look lovely, Alexis." His voice sounded rough. "Happy birthday."

Alexis shot John a cutting look. He grinned. Her brother was going to get an earful in a few minutes.

John turned toward Luke. "Why don't you join us? We're going to Caccatori's. It's not far."

Alexis swung his way, stifling the words that jumped to her tongue. Sharee's eyes rounded.

Luke tilted his head toward Alexis. "I wouldn't dream of infringing on your birthday dinner. John's been overseas too long, forgotten his etiquette."

"As a matter of fact—" John started.

"And I'm certainly not dressed to match Alexis' dress. Or Sharee's. But thanks for the invitation." He moved off.

John elbowed Alexis and mouthed at her, "Ask him." She shook her head, and John frowned and mouthed another question. "Why not?"

Alexis glared.

"Ask him." John mouthed once more.

Alexis crossed her arms over her chest but looked Luke's way. He punched his key fob, and the truck lights blinked.

"Luke." Her voice sounded weak. She cleared her throat. "Luke."

He turned. "Alexis, I'm not going to crash your birthday dinner."

"You...you won't. Please come."

He aimed his frown between her and John. "As I said, I'm not dressed."

"You look comfortable. Your boots and jeans are fine."

"Next to you..."

"If I don't mind, you shouldn't."

He glowered at her.

She straightened. "Of course, if you really don't want to…"

His glower increased. "That's not it."

"Then come."

"We'll have to go in two trucks," John said. "Do you know the way?"

Luke's eyes narrowed. "Yes."

Alexis grinned at his tone. Her conniving brother could be in trouble on two fronts tonight. John grabbed Sharee's hand and led her around to the passenger side of his truck. Alexis switched her purse's strap from one shoulder to the other and waited.

Luke shook his head but put out his hand. She walked toward him. He caught her fingers, led her around to the passenger door, and opened it for her.

"You don't have to be pushed into this, Alexis. I'll drop you off and leave."

"Oh, I think it will be fun if we're both there to give John a little trouble."

The side of his mouth quirked. "Do you?"

"Yes. Definitely."

"If you're sure."

She squeezed his hand and climbed into the cab. "I'm sure."

❧

Luke pushed his plate away, sat back and watched Alexis as she talked with Sharee. He'd enjoyed the food and the conversation, but watching Alexis talk and laugh and tease had satisfied him more – even if he had to do that while answering her brother's questions about his life and his Christianity.

The reason for John's invitation became clear not long after the first course arrived. His peripheral vision caught Sharee's squeeze on her husband's arm as the questions became too personal for such short acquaintance.

He winked at Sharee. "My life is an open book. In fact, you and John are welcome to drop by my place sometime and ride or just enjoy the scenery." He glanced at Alexis with a mocking smile. "In fact, Alexis will be glad to bring you and let you feed the horses."

"I—" Alexis only got one word out.

John's voice broke across hers. "Why does it sound like there is a whole story in that one sentence?"

Luke let his grin widen.

Alexis sent him a glance that he knew would start a fire if they had the right kindling.

"He thinks he's being cute. It's a very harmless story."

John glanced from one to the other. "Oh?"

"I just wanted to take some pictures. Of the leaves, you know. All the yellows, reds, and golds. It's so different here than it is in Florida."

"You didn't get enough of that in Atlanta?"

Alexis waved her hand in dismissal. "I always had some case that seemed to keep me busy from dawn to dusk. I hardly ever saw daylight. So, I was really looking forward to getting here and having time to relax and enjoy life." Her voice struggled over the last few words. John's hand covered hers. Luke sent John an inquisitive look, but John gave a slight shake of his head.

"Anyway," Alexis continued. "I was out driving and saw this beautiful horse running along the road. I had to stop and get a picture." Luke coughed, and Alexis speared him with a look. "I just happened to have some carrots and when Max came up to me..."

"That's the horse?" Sharee asked. "Had he gotten loose or something?"

"No, not loose. He was inside the fence, but he came when I called."

Luke leaned forward. "You enticed him with a carrot."

"I did not."

"You did. He doesn't go to strangers."

"Well, he came to me. He came when I called, and I was barely inside the fence."

"Inside?" He turned in his seat and gave her a more direct look. *"Inside?"*

"I, uh…"

Her brother shifted toward them. "Wasn't she supposed to be inside?"

A flush started on Alexis' face. "That has nothing to do with it. The horse came right to me. I petted him, and I did have some carrots, so I gave him some." She shrugged. "I can't help it if he likes me."

"Except for the big 'No Trespassing' signs up and down the whole fence." Luke watched the flush climb higher and held his grin back. He'd better get her off the hook. "Well, she's not lying about Max liking her. He does. So does my dog."

"A dog? What kind of dog?" John's voice quickened, and Sharee laughed.

"Is that funny?"

"Only John's reaction. He misses his. We had to give him away when we went to Indonesia."

Luke tilted his head at John. "That would be hard. What kind?"

"A Lab. Yours?"

"Blue Heeler."

"From Australia?"

"Developed in Australia for driving cattle."

John nodded then his look flicked back to Alexis. "So, I take it the horse you saw belongs to Luke, and that you've been out to his place a couple of times."

Luke wanted to laugh. Her brother had all the marks of a warden. "She's only been once. But Max kicked a hole in the barn, and Alexis helped with the other horses and later with Max when the vet came. And Farley just left me and stayed with her the whole day."

"It had rained so much the night before—"

Luke caught her hand and squeezed. She stopped and turned toward him. He gave her hand another quick squeeze. Did she see where she was going? Telling her brother about the night before would lead to the fact that she'd spent the night. That might not generate the sort of warmth Luke was hoping to gain here. "Let's just say, since the animals all love her, she's welcome to take as many pictures as she wants at my place."

John's glance jumped from Luke to his sister and back. The silence grew until Alexis turned toward Sharee.

"So, the doctors were completely wrong about Johnnie?"

Sharee nodded and smiled. "God is still in the miracle business." She looked across at Luke. "I had just gone into labor when Alexis called. Such an awful time. Their dad dying, and me in labor. John couldn't get home, and he finally—"

Luke's hand hadn't left hers. It tightened again. "Your dad died? When?"

She pulled away, shifting in her chair. "Five months ago."

The words were so low he had to strain to hear them. His gaze jumped to John. "Your father?"

"Yes."

"I'm sorry. I didn't know."

Waves of pain came from Alexis. He could feel them, and that startled him. He wanted to gather her to him, but didn't move.

"I'm sorry," Sharee said. "I assumed you knew."

"No. I..." He thought about how solemn Alexis seemed. So little laughter - until tonight. "I'm sorry, Alexis. You've had a rough time. Moving, a new career – all of that is stressful. On top of your dad passing. Was he a Christian?"

She hesitated a moment before turning to her brother.

"Yes." John's eyes focused on Alexis as if she had asked the question. "I led him to the Lord the night before we flew to Indonesia."

A frown appeared on Alexis' face. "He never said anything."

"Dad wouldn't. Unless he felt the timing was right."

Luke sensed the undercurrents but couldn't define them. Why did Alexis look upset? Shouldn't she be ecstatic with the news? Didn't she believe it?

Sharee leaned toward him. "That was the only thing that made being away anywhere near acceptable."

"You and John were overseas when it happened?"

"Yes." John's gaze searched his sister's. He put his arm around Sharee and pulled her closer. "We're missionaries. Sharee went into labor not two hours before Alexis called. I couldn't leave her. I couldn't make it home to see Dad, couldn't make it to the funeral, couldn't help Alexis." The roughness of his voice exposed the pain and frustration with which he'd dealt.

"It's all right, John." Alexis leaned forward. "I knew you had to be with Sharee."

Her brother leaned toward her. "But you had to do everything. Upholding Mom and Dad's new wife. And yourself."

Luke groaned inside. Some of that reunion he'd seen made sense now. "His death was a surprise?"

John raised his head and met Luke's gaze. *Grief there, too.*

"Yes. A heart attack." When Luke nodded, John continued. "Sharee's labor lasted two days. I had to threaten to take the hospital apart before they would do a cesarean. When Johnnie was born, they told us that because of complications, he might not ever see or hear or walk."

"But God—" Sharee said.

"Yes. Johnnie was in intensive care, and we went every day and prayed. And the church we were members of and the people we had ministered to began showing up at the hospital and praying around the clock. Finally, the doctors said to take him home. I think they wanted to get rid of us and the prayer circles, but that's the best thing we could have done. As soon as he was home, he began making progress. We know he can see and hear. He moves his legs just fine. God healed him." His eyes left Luke's face and focused on Alexis. "God is the same, yesterday, today and forever."

"That's true." Luke said. He sat back in his chair. "Praise God for your miracle."

John's face lifted, his eyes shone. "We did. And then we came home as soon as we knew he could travel."

"So where is he?"

"With Sharee's mom and dad. They drove up to be here for a few days. We rented a cabin on the mountain. Beautiful view. My mom is driving down. We'll go back home to Florida in a week or two." His eyes focused on his sister. "I wanted to see Alexis first."

&

Luke placed another log on the fire, set the screen in front of it, and backed away. Farley circled and went to find a place to sleep. No storms tonight, so he let the Blue Heeler inside. The sparks in the fireplace rose and glowed. He watched until the flames burned steady then eased into the recliner.

He'd enjoyed the evening. No surprise. Alexis had relaxed, and she, her brother, and sister-in-law had proved warm, witty and good company. Even the late revelation of her father's death had not kept all laughter from the group. On the drive back to her car, she'd acted skittish again, like Sandy when Mandy wasn't near. He wondered what about him made her nervous.

The fire's warmth massaged him. He stretched his arms over his head and clasped his wrists with his hands. She looked gorgeous in the dress. He smiled for a moment then brought his arms down, crossed them over his chest and chewed the inside of his cheek.

Beautiful women are trouble, Lord. You and I talked about this. I'm no Adonis. The only thing I've got going for me is this place and You. I'm not ready to get involved with someone who might leave. Not another one.

If he didn't want to get involved, why had he asked her over this week? At dinner, she mentioned that she'd love to be around when he let Max loose. And since he had no other birthday gift to give her, he'd invited her. That was the reason. The only reason.

Yeah.

Right.

And the moon was made of pepper-jack cheese.

Chapter 9

She stepped into the foyer as he closed the door behind her. "Thank you for letting me come."

"I didn't think I could keep you away." He gave her a slow smile.

Alexis smiled back, feeling that strange warmth that his smile brought some times. "He's been boxed up for so long, I just wanted to see him take off when you let him out."

"Well, he's been in the corral a couple of times this week, but I understand what you mean." He looked down at her feet. "Real boots."

"I had to unpack the rest of my boxes to find them. These were my favorites. I never thought I'd wear them again."

"Well, riding is great exercise. You should start again."

"If it's such good exercise, what's with the exercise room down the hall?" When he said nothing, she wondered if she'd overstepped some invisible line. "I saw it the first night I was here."

"I set up all the equipment when I first moved in, but I don't use it much. There's enough to be done around here to keep fit."

She nodded and tried not to look toward his chest. He wore a T-shirt with an unbuttoned long-sleeve flannel shirt over it. He looked good, workouts or not. And since when had she cared about a guy's physique?

Her eyes met his, and the heat rose in her face.

"What about you?" He asked, leaving her to wonder if he'd noticed her glance. "What do you do for exercise since you don't ride?"

"I used to work out most workday evenings. I had to get rid of the tension after court or working on a case. It helped my thinking, too. But lately, I haven't done much." She glanced out the kitchen window. "And you're right, I remember that working around a place like this can keep you in shape. Not just riding, but lifting bales of hay and fifty pound bags of feed, climbing fences, all that kind of stuff."

"Unless you're the type of person that thrives on gym-toned, bulked-up bodies, this type of exercise is fine."

His voice carried an undertone it hadn't before. She studied his face, wondering. After a moment, she said, "Why don't you use the room for something else then?"

He ran a hand through his hair. "Good idea. I thought I needed it when I moved here. Teresa would have insisted." His eyes focused on the kitchen window.

"Teresa?"

"My ex."

"Oh." She wasn't sure what to say. He'd been married before. "No children?"

"No. She didn't want to mess up her body. She got very body-conscious sometime while I was overseas."

"Oh."

"And the war didn't help."

Alexis had heard that tone from witnesses before. He was trying to tell her something without actually saying it, which meant the clues were there. She'd know what he was saying if she thought about it. Her gaze dropped to his leg then rose again.

"Your limp?"

"My leg."

She frowned. "Tell me."

"You don't know?"

"What should I know?"

He said nothing just searched her face. At last, he stepped forward and pulled a chair from the kitchen table. "Thought someone would have mentioned it."

He tugged the boot off and rolled up the left pant leg of his jeans. The plastic and metal foot and then the leg appeared. A prosthetic.

She choked down the lump in her throat, gripped the back of the chair. "Oh, Luke. I'm so sorry."

"I was, too, at first. You have to get past it. Teresa couldn't."

Her look jumped from the prosthesis back to his face. She knew her mouth hung open. "Luke, I...I..."

He waved his hand. "It's okay."

"How...?"

"The war. Bomb went off. Lost my foot, part of my leg below the knee. It's called a BKA, below-the-knee amputation."

She wanted to ask some questions, but his tone told her to wait. She stared at his leg. "It's not okay." She heard the staccato sound of her voice and wanted to say more. "Your wife was a Christian?"

"No one's perfect. You know that. There was only one that was perfect."

So she'd heard. *Jesus*. They all brought it back to Jesus. She started to shake her head, but didn't. "It doesn't make it right."

He smiled and rolled the material back down over the prosthetic. "With the leg change, came other changes. After a while, I stopped working out so hard, stopped trying to prove I was still a man. Our outlooks on what was important began to differ."

She sat down across from him. What had he gone through? Wasn't losing a leg enough? How could his wife just leave? She put a tentative hand on his arm. "The possession of a leg does not make you a man, and losing a leg doesn't make you less of one. The tragedy, though, can make you bitter or better."

His gaze dropped to her hand and rose again to her face. She moved her hand, wondering if she'd overstepped another boundary. She'd overstepped her own. How long had it been since she'd touched a man in some kind of communication? Besides John and her dad, it had been years.

He bent down and pulled on the boot. "Sounds like you're speaking from experience."

"Maybe."

He said nothing. The silence stretched.

He'd told her about his wife, shown her his leg; but could she trust him? She'd opened up to another man, and it had ended in disaster. She stood up and walked to the back door.

"Maybe later?" he asked from behind her.

"Maybe," she said, not meaning it at all.

His gaze followed her as she hurried down the steps, putting space between them. He'd felt the tenderness when she touched him. Not something he'd noticed but once or twice before and only with Jessica.

So, something had happened. He'd guessed that already. Something with a man. Something that made her bitter whether she realized it or not. It hadn't ruined her – yet – but still influenced her in a deep way.

He watched her walk ahead of him, admiring her tall, model-like build. She wore jeans and a loose t-shirt – nothing suggestive or provocative. Her long hair swung and caught the light. He smiled. She added a nice touch to his place.

Luke lengthened his stride until he was next to her. He squashed the sudden urge to take her hand, and they reached the barn together. The stallion stretched his head over the half-door. Farley ran from some hidden place in the barn and circled their feet. Luke patted his head.

"Keeping him company, boy?"

The dog sniffed Alexis' hand before scratching at Max's door.

"Let me check him first." Luke pushed the dog away, slipped into the stall and walked to the stallion's side. He lifted the horse's hind foot, running his hand over the shaved portion of the leg, over stitches that still showed. "Looks good. The vet said he'll do fine."

Alexis reached over the door and palmed the horse's nose. "How you doing, big boy? Ready to get out of here?"

"More than ready, I'm sure." Luke came forward and slipped a lead rope from a hook then clipped it on the horse's halter. "Would you mind standing near the mares? I brought them in early because I planned to let him go, but he might decide they're more interesting than a run in the field. Just shoo him toward the door if he looks that way."

"Men are always so double-minded," Alexis said, moving toward the end of the barn. Both mares had their noses over their doors. "We should have brought some carrots."

"The girls are getting big enough without extra treats."

"Oh, yeah. Says the man that brings the biggest carrots I've ever seen for the stallion."

Luke laughed. "I bought him first. Guess he's my favorite."

"It's not noticeable or anything."

He sent her an amused look and opened the door. "Here we go."

The horse shoved him back into the middle of the barn and danced forward. Farley barked and slipped between them.

"Farley, out! Come on, Max."

He led the horse into the sunlight and toward the gate. The horse's excitement caused him to tighten his hold to keep them both at a walk.

"Alexis, get the gate, will you? He seems to know what's going on."

She scooted past them, giving a wide berth to the stallion, and unlatched the gate. It swung open.

"Back out of the way."

She moved to the side, and Luke grinned as they passed her then stopped and unclipped the lead rope.

"There you go, Max. Head out."

The stallion shoved his shoulder into him, and Luke stumbled backward but caught himself before the horse shook his head and trotted free.

"Let's close the gate before he decides this side of the fence looks better."

They pushed it closed and turned in time to see Maximus take a long stride, stretch out and race for the hilltop, mane flying.

Alexis laughed. "Wow. Look at him go." She moved forward, her gaze on the horse. The stallion disappeared on the other side of the hill. "He's probably going to be running along the road again." Raising her arms, she caught her hair, twirled it, and pulled it on top of her head. The fine hairs at her neck were dark with perspiration.

Luke caught his breath and cleared his throat. "Probably."

"And some tourist will want to stop and take pictures." She turned toward him, a smile teasing her features.

The sight of Max running free had thrilled him as it did her, but the sight of her bare neck and her closeness stirred other feelings. His heart kicked into a staccato beat, and he raised his hands to rest on her shoulders.

"Alexis." His hands tightened; his voice roughened. Her muscles bunched under his hands, and he bent and kissed the side of her neck.

She jerked away, her eyes wide and dilated. His did the same at her look. If he'd ever seen fear – and the war overseas had made sure he had – he was seeing it now. He took a step back.

She was afraid of him? She'd stayed the night of the storm and found she was safe, so why was she afraid now? His mind grappled for some explanation while they stared at each other. Afraid of a relationship? With an amputee? Although she hadn't acted that way earlier, hadn't acted horrified or disgusted.

His mind rested on the one thing he knew. Friendship and a romantic involvement were two different things. Teresa had made that clear. She wanted a friendship, she'd told him, and a divorce. Not a marriage, a friendship.

He took another step away. "Sorry. I was out of line."

Alexis said nothing.

She's struggling. Still. He wanted to say, "Hey, don't worry about it. It's okay." But those words stuck in his throat. Instead, he said, "I know you need to get back. I'll get your purse."

The walk to the house took forever, his mind whirling, coping with the disappointment that knuckled a hollow place into his stomach. Her purse sat on the kitchen table. He grabbed it…and stopped.

The weight was twice or three times what he'd expected. What did she keep in the thing? He fingered the side of the bag, lifted a brow, and probed the heaviness again.

She carried a gun?

Chapter 10

After she left, he walked back to the house, went down the hall to the exercise room and stood in the doorway. He had tried for awhile to be everything Teresa wanted. If he couldn't give her back his leg, he could at least give her the chest and shoulders of a man in whom she could be proud. But that was before he learned of the affair she'd had while he was overseas, while he was still whole.

After the divorce, after moving, he'd kept at the exercise for awhile. One day, God entered the room through the window's dancing light – entered the room and spoke, not in an audible voice, but for him it had the same effect. The knowledge that he was okay just as he was sunk deep into his being, changing him. Since that time, life had settled into a deep contentment. Yes, the house seemed lonely once in awhile, but he knew it wouldn't be forever. He'd been content to wait.

Alexis had changed that. He told God he wanted someone who laughed, and who wasn't pretty. Alexis was pretty, and she didn't laugh. Well, not until her birthday dinner and then again today. That's what had startled him, drew him. She'd laughed. And she'd touched him.

Her rejection slapped like a twelve-foot wave in pounding surf. His handling of it stunk. He knew that. He'd handed her purse to her and let her drive away without saying another word.

His throat worked, and his eyes shifted and focused on the equipment in the room. He shouldn't be here. He couldn't prove he was still a man here.

Go. Go ride instead. Shovel manure. Fork hay. Don't stay here.

But he stepped through the doorway and picked up a barbell he hadn't touched in months. Working on the property and with the animals really did keep him in shape. Just not sculpted, gym-toned, muscle-bound shape like Teresa wanted. And maybe like Alexis wanted.

It won't make up for a missing leg.

Yeah, but at least I can wear myself out.

He hefted the barbell, rolled it toward him all the while staring at the weight bench. Leaning over, he picked up the barbell's mate and rolled it to his chest, too. Then he put them down and stepped to the weight bench.

At least, I can wear myself out.

Alexis rested her elbows on the dining table and put her head in her hands. She had returned from her morning jog to find the condo empty. That should ring all kind of warning bells. Instead, it sent relief zipping through her. She'd worry about where Jessica and her mom went later.

She took a shower, did her hair, put on her make-up, and dressed.

Her heart still stuttered when she thought of Luke's mouth on her neck, his hands on her arms. Fear had seized her as soon as he touched her. The intimacy in his touch, its gentleness, shook her. If he hadn't kissed her neck, she might have managed.

But Brock's kiss… Why couldn't she get past that? She'd trusted him, and now another man wanted her trust. Sure. Right. And how do I know you're any different?

Luke's face rose in front of her. His shock and then shut-down made everything worse. What had she done to him? She'd never had that kind of influence or effect on anyone unless it was in the courtroom. Not in a personal way.

She stood and walked into the living area. He'd told her

about his ex-wife. He'd opened himself to her. Could she ever do that with another human being? Besides John?

John would tell her to give Luke a chance, give love a chance. But she'd tried that before. She swung around and stared at the tasteful furnishings, the ones she had picked out when she moved here, the sculpture, the paintings. Start over, she'd told herself. But had she? Hadn't she brought the same problems with her to Tennessee?

Bitter or better, she said to Luke. Where was she on that continuum? Maybe, she needed a fresh perspective on life...and on men.

The front door opened. Voices bounced down the hall, and she stuffed the feelings that had escaped back inside. Forcing a smile, she turned toward the door.

Jessica carried bags of groceries but her look mirrored how Alexis imagined her own face looked a few moments ago.

What was wrong?

She stepped forward, taking a bag from the girl's arms. Behind her, Dawn yanked the door closed.

"I can't believe how much everything cost these days! Prices are getting higher than ever."

"Mom." Jessica glared over her shoulder.

They all three crowded into the kitchen. Alexis glanced around. Space adequate for her did not mean space adequate for three. She set her bag on the island counter in the center. The other two did the same.

Their agreement included sharing the expenses for food. Everything else Alexis would cover. Dawn still had her job, but she also had her own mortgage and bills to pay.

"Don't worry, Jessica. I know just what your mom means. Prices are going up all the time." She pulled bananas and strawberries out of the bag. "These look good. It's amazing how we can get everything at anytime of the year now. That's one reason food costs more. We don't have to wait for a Florida spring to get strawberries."

"Why wait for spring?" Jessica asked, loading the

refrigerator with chicken breasts and broccoli and tomatoes.

Dawn rolled her eyes. "Young people know nothing these days." She took a loaf of bread and set it on a back counter near the coffee machine and toaster.

"Whoa! Look at this! Somebody had a chocolate craving." Alexis smiled and handed Dawn the chocolate cake. "Jess, strawberries get ripe in late winter or early spring. That's nature's time for them to ripen. These days, growers force growth and ripen them no matter what time of year it is. But in Florida when I was a kid, the Strawberry Festival and the strawberries were our first signs of spring. You could get all the strawberry shortcake you could eat there."

"Really? What else did they have?"

"What *do* they have? It still goes on each year. Lots of food, animals, music, crafts."

Dawn grabbed the plastic bags and started for the trash can.

"Oh. Let me have those." Alexis put out a hand. "I'll recycle them back at the store."

"Yeah, yeah. We do some of that, too. I'm not thinking." They moved down the hall to the living area. Dawn dropped onto the couch. "The meeting with the prosecutor just fried me. Like filing the complaint. Can you believe what they put you through to report a crime?"

Alexis sat in the barrel-shaped chair. Her gaze flicked to Jessica's pinched face as she curled up at the opposite end of the sofa from her mom.

"Is this really worth it?" The decibels in Dawn's voice climbed. "And since Leland's not in jail, they can wait up to thirty days to have a preliminary hearing."

Alexis sat straighter. "It is a long, tedious process sometimes. But if we don't prosecute criminals in this country, we give way to lawlessness."

She looked at Jessica. "Do you want Leland to get away with what he did to you? Would you want him to do this to someone else?"

The girl shook her head. "You know I don't. It's just frustrating."

Her mom leaned forward. "They haven't found Leland yet, and they probably won't."

"And the prosecutor said he'd be out on bail in no time." Jessica's shoulders slumped. "Mom said even if we get that Order of Protection, he can still come after me. It's just a piece of paper."

Alexis kept her focus on the girl but wondered what else Dawn had said. "I'm sure Leland knows the consequences of breaking the order."

"They can't find him, anyway."

"They will. The police are good at that, even if it takes some time."

"How long, though? And how long until it's all finished?"

"I can't tell you, Honey. Laws are different from state to state, and each county's procedures can be different too."

Jessica slouched back on the couch and threw a look at her mom. "It might be easier to just forget it. I don't know if...I can go through with it." Her voice broke.

"Awe, Jess." Alexis wanted to slip from her chair, kneel in front of the girl and hug her; but the scowl on her mom's face kept Alexis in her seat.

Instead, Dawn scooted to the edge of the sofa. "I'm thinking of my girl here. What's she gonna get out of this? Just trouble. And ain't she got enough as it is? And what's she going to do with this baby?"

"Mom, it's okay." Jessica sniffed and wiped at her eyes.

"See what I mean?" Dawn leaned over and reached for Jessica's hand.

Alexis' gaze moved from one to the other. Their feelings didn't surprise her. She knew how the shock, denial, anger, and bitterness would have to work through Jessica's life before she could deal with what had happened and move forward with her life. Her pregnancy after the rape compounded the situation, but she'd seen other women make a clear decision to fight back, to join a cause, or go on to college – in a sense, take back their lives. She'd also seen women return to the same situation they were in. Jessica, she felt sure, would fit the first category, if her mother did not undermine the girl's strengths.

"Jess, have you thought about the counseling I recommended?"

"Jessica doesn't have money for counseling."

Alexis shot her mom a surprised look. "I thought I made that clear at the hospital. She won't be charged at the rape counseling center or at the college. It's free. And the Christian pregnancy center Jessica went to, they'll give referrals for help with the baby."

Dawn sent Alexis another scowl, but said nothing.

What were the undercurrents she sensed? Was it the baby? Leland? Or more? Between classes, John's return, and then yesterday's debacle with Luke, what had she missed?

Her eyes rested on Jessica. The girl could handle it. Almost everyone wavered.

৵

Alexis walked down the hall from her office and forced her shoulders back. A nervous hand went to her upswept hair. Facing Luke caused more trepidation in her than the hurricane heading for Florida today. When she saw the news, it cheered her to think that John, Sharee, and the baby were safely snuggled in a cabin here in Tennessee. Her mom and Sharee's parents were close by, too. She took a long breath and entered his classroom.

Luke's eyes shifted, and he straightened – a mirror image of her own action a minute ago. The students glanced her way. Some nodded a hello. No one said anything. She slipped to the back of the classroom and sat in an empty desk.

A long couple of days had passed. She hadn't seen him, although his voice had drifted into her office as he taught.

The sound of it hurt her, and knowing she'd wounded him made the pain harder to stomach.

Over the lasts couple of weeks, she'd caught small portions of his teaching on Isaiah. It surprised her that one book in the Bible could take so much time to cover. But from what she heard, he seemed to relate it to other sections of the Bible, interweaving the significance of the different books.

The class had five more minutes. She sat back to listen.

Luke's glance slid over her, his face tightening before he looked back at the students and continued teaching. "In the midst of the prophecy of God's judgment on Israel - for not following His ways and worshipping other gods - Isaiah shows us that God is still in the redemption business, before and after Christ. He points often to the coming Messiah.

"Chapter nine, of course, is only one place of many where Isaiah brings in messianic prophecy. He says that the light has shined on the people that dwell in the shadow of death. The light. A reference to Christ. Psalms twenty-three also talks about the shadow of death and points to God's goodness in the midst of it. God inspired the scriptures and tells us repeatedly about his love, his mercy, and his redemption.

"Verse six of chapter nine is the popular scripture, the one we hear at Christmas, 'For unto us a child is born, to us a son is given, and the government will be on his shoulders. And he will be called Wonderful Counselor, Mighty God, Everlasting Father, Prince of Peace.' The reference to Jesus is clear. The Trinity – three in one – is presented."

A student raised his hand, and when Luke nodded at him, he said, "I'm not sure how you get that. I see the Father and the Son. We know the reference to the Prince of Peace is Jesus. Where is the Holy Spirit?"

"The Counselor. The Holy Spirit is our counselor. In John 14:26, Jesus tells his disciples that it is good that he is leaving, for then the Counselor will come. And he says exactly whom he means – the Holy Spirit. The books of Luke and Romans also mention the Holy Spirit as counselor and as teacher. Of course, He is more than that. The Holy Spirit represents the power of God. When we talk about being born again, born from above, we are talking about the Holy Spirit. Jesus referred to this in John three. Believing causes rebirth and new life."

The words "new life" caught Alexis' attention. Isn't that why she moved here? To get a new life? Strange. She was sure what Luke referred to had nothing to do with the type of life she was seeking. Still, a strange coincidence.

Luke looked down at his watch. "We've strayed off course a little. Remember what your homework is. I'll see you tomorrow."

A couple of heads turned her way, but Alexis just smiled; and the students exited. Talk would follow her visit to Luke's room, but she couldn't help that.

Luke shoved papers and books into his backpack. Even with the tension crackling between them, she almost smiled. His backpack, her briefcase; his jeans, her business suit. He hadn't worn a suit since the first day of classes. They were different, just like their beliefs.

"Tell me about this new life." Alexis said. "Why are you jumping from Isaiah to John to Romans?"

His hands stopped, and he raised his head. The green eyes focused on hers, and the pause lasted seconds too long.

She shifted in her chair. "Well?"

He grabbed the Bible sitting on the desk, shoved it into the bag and zipped it closed. "Is that a real question?"

"What?" He'd thrown her. "Why wouldn't it be?"

A line formed between his brows. "I'm sure you know God's plan for salvation was in place before he created the world. He knew Adam and Eve would sin, that the human race would need saving. From Genesis to Revelation, the Bible is full of predictions and prophesies about that, about Jesus."

Alexis frowned. Was that an answer to her question? She'd never heard that before, never thought about it. God knew from the beginning? She wanted to ask another question but too many would show her complete ignorance on the subject. Maybe she needed to read the Bible herself. She'd bought one after they hired her, just in case. Maybe she should read Isaiah. How hard could it be to understand?

She slipped out of the desk. This wasn't why she'd come. "Max is doing okay?"

"Yes."

The terseness of his answer caused her stomach to clench. She cleared her throat. "We need to talk."

"I told you I was out of line. Let's leave it at that." He slipped the backpack's straps through his arms.

She rose and stepped toward the door, blocking his exit. "Would you stop, please?"

He stilled.

"You...you surprised me Saturday, but my reaction had nothing to do with you personally...with who you are. It's me." She hesitated, drew a breath. "Can we pretend it never happened? Can we just go back to the moment we let Max out and start again?"

He said nothing. The line between his brows deepened.

She stared at him, thinking and discarding a number of things she wanted to say. She waved her hands. "Luke, I'm going out of my way here, way out of my comfort zone. Would you help, please?"

"I'm not sure what you want, Alexis."

Her hands dropped. *What did she want?* "I don't know either."

"You don't? I can't see you winning many cases that way."

Annoyed, she focused on the green eyes. "No, I wouldn't win cases this way, but that has nothing to do with this."

The silence grew between them.

He broke it after a minute. "If you're serious, come watch the soccer game in an hour. Faculty versus students. You should be there to cheer us on, anyway."

"Us? You play?"

Her surprise escaped before she could stop it.

He stepped around her and out the door. "Yes, Alexis, I do."

Chapter 11

Luke changed into athletic shorts, a sweat-wicking shirt, and soccer cleats; and, for the first time in years, wondered how he looked. It didn't matter. He'd told her to come to the game so he could see her reaction. He wasn't sure, and neither was she, what she wanted; but she would not be able to get around his leg, or lack of it, this way.

Yeah, Alexis, I play soccer. And more.

He stuffed his jeans and shirt into the backpack, picked up his boots and headed for the parking lot.

Of course, he had surprised the other faculty members, too, two years ago when he showed up for practice. They let him play, but no one was too sure about it until he kicked his first goal – one of three that day. Someone had coined his nickname then. "Metalballer." The name stuck.

He threw his boots and backpack onto the floorboard of his truck and headed to the field.

The cool autumn day shifted toward evening. He glanced upward. The sky's intense blue had silvered, and it wouldn't be long before the field lights came on.

Along the sidelines, students, faculty, and staff set up camp chairs and other seating. The team warmed up on the field. He joined them.

Six on the team had played soccer in either high school or college. Himself included. He'd played in both before the war. Each year, the students on the college team showed over-confidence in themselves by their lack of practice beforehand. A few plays into the game, they always realized their mistake.

Not long after the faculty team's warm-up, the game started. Alexis hadn't made an appearance. Disappointment slipped over him.

Give her a few more minutes.

He shrugged off the regret and sent the ball careening to Thomas Hartley. He and Tom and Don played forward. Tom caught it and sent it on to Don. Luke ran past him, heading downfield. The ball flew past, and Tom caught it, tried for a goal, and missed. Luke stopped, breathing hard, feeling the coolness in the air drying the sweat in his shirt.

She hadn't shown. He hadn't pictured her as someone who would not keep her word.

Don sent the ball his way. Luke caught it, skirted two defenders, and sent it slicing toward the goal with as much force as he had. It whizzed by the goalie before the man could get an arm in the air. The sidelines erupted, and Don clapped him on the shoulder when he went by.

"Wondered if you were with us today."

"Metalballer!" Someone yelled. "Metalballer is back!"

At halftime, they headed for the sidelines and something to drink. He'd scored their only goal, and his teammates pounded his back. Shoving aside the acute disappointment, he bantered back and forth with them and reached inside the cooler for some Gatorade.

"Here." Don shook damp, black hair from his eyes and handed Luke a dripping bottle. "I'll give you the first half, but I plan to out score you in the second."

Alexis popped up from a blanket on the ground and stood smiling at him. He missed Don's handoff, and the plastic bottle hit his prosthetic foot and rolled across her Asics tennis shoes.

She was here.

Alexis scooped it up and handed it back to him. "You're good."

She'd changed clothes. Instead of her gray suit, she wore a pair of jeans and a t-shirt. An open fleece jacket in turquoise highlighted her coffee-colored eyes. The dark hair fell loose around her shoulders. She grinned at him. His heart kicked. Where had she come from? How had he missed her?

Don glanced back and forth between them. "Of course, if you're distracted that won't be much of a problem."

Luke's focus shifted from Alexis to Don. He grinned. "Distracted or not, I'll take that challenge."

"What?" Alexis' voice jumped before she could stop it.

Jessica stepped back, rubbed her hands down her jeans. "I'm withdrawing the complaint, and I'm not going to testify."

The words slammed Alexis like one of Luke's kicks past the goalie. She lowered herself into the barrel chair. Jessica had blurted the words as soon as she'd walked into the room.

She wanted to ask the question again, but the word wouldn't form.

"Mom went home to get the house ready. She said for me to come home when I told you, and that I never should have gone to the hospital. That you...you had no right to call the police. That I should have talked with her first."

Alexis wanted to put a hand out and say, "Stop. Wait." This week's ocean of emotions already had enough rolling breakers. The serious high she'd had from dinner with Luke and the team crashed, the words shattering her mood like waves smashing a boardwalk during a hurricane.

An acid taste rose in her mouth. She'd heard these words too many times. It wouldn't help to lash out at the girl. This was her mother's doing. And the woman had abandoned Jessica to give Alexis the news.

She drew her tongue across her top lip. "Do you mind telling me why? Do you want him to get away with what he did to you?"

"Of course not! He convinced Mom that I exaggerated the whole thing, that I lied."

"Exaggerated?" Alexis tried to keep her voice level. "Exaggerated the rape? Exaggerated beating you and keeping you locked up all day? Jessica, he didn't just—"

The girl's hands jumped out from her sides. "I know all that! You don't have to tell me. But mom believes…" The girl's voice dissolved. She dropped her head. "She…she believes Leland. Not me."

Alexis' anger melted. She stepped forward and enfolded the girl in her arms. Her own emotions could wait. She rested her head against Jessica's wet cheek. *How could a mother do this to her daughter?* But she'd heard it before.

"We…we were always so close until Leland moved in." Jessica's voice filled with tears.

"You will be again, Jess. Give it time. Besides, once you've started this process, it's no longer yours to continue. Your mother may not want Leland to be charged with a crime, but it is now in the District Attorney's hands."

"But what if I don't testify?" Jessica sniffed and drew away. "Mother told me to withdraw the complaint and not to testify."

"It's out of our hands. And you had a rape test, remember? They have the evidence." She wouldn't tell the girl how much they needed her testimony to ensure a conviction. "Your mother is not thinking this through. I suspected she'd talked with Leland. What did he tell her?"

"That I tried to seduce him. That I got undressed just to entice him, and that he locked me in the room and was waiting until she got there – so that she could deal with me."

"That will all be disproved once we get the rape test results. And I was there, remember? I'll testify and Professor Stephens will, too."

Jessica leaned her head back against Alexis' shoulder. The tears started again. "I don't know if it will matter. Leland will think of something else to tell her. And, Professor Jergenson?"

"Yes?"

"Mom thinks I should get an abortion."

ↀ

Bam. Bam. Bam.

The sound echoed throughout the house. Luke stared into the darkness and rolled over in bed to see the clock. The fluorescent glow showed after midnight.

Bam. Bam. Bam.

What in the world? Who would pound his door this time of night? Whoever it was, whatever it was, it had to be important. He sat up and leaned forward. Grabbing the crutches that leaned against the dresser, he slipped his arms into the cuffs, stood and made his way to the living room.

Bam. Bam. Bam.

When he checked the side window, surprise ricocheted through him. He flipped the lock on the door and swung it wide. "Alexis?"

Her arms were crossed over her chest, hands clutching each forearm, the car keys dangling from one fist. "I'm sorry, I..." Her eyes darted to his crutches then dropped to his leg.

He opened the door wider and limped backward.

Her gaze rose to meet his. "You...are you okay?"

"Yes. Come in." The flannels he wore tonight had one leg cut off below the stump. That look jolted most people into his reality, and Alexis had never seen him with the crutches, either. He focused on her a moment then closed the door. "I don't wear the prosthetic at night. I use the forearm crutches if I have to get up."

Her eyes dropped again. "You didn't that first night."

"Because I knew you'd wake at some point. I waited." And this discussion could wait, too. Something else had forced her from the warmth and safety of her condo. "What's wrong?"

"I..." She brought her gaze back to his. "Jessica. The baby. I..."

"Is she okay?"

"Yes. I..."

"The baby?"

"Yes. For now. Her mom's been pushing for an abortion, though. I just found out tonight. Plus. I..." She stopped.

He bent his head, saw the moisture start around her eyes. The urge to pull her into his arms flooded him. He dropped his focus to the crutches, fought the frustration. "Come sit down. The fire's barely alive, but I'll stoke it."

He let her precede him into the room and find a chair – the same one she'd slept in the night of the storm. She curled up in it and put her head down. He went to the fire.

She'd come all this way in the middle of the night – to him. The thought both warmed and bothered him. What had happened?

When the flames began to jump, he turned and studied her. Her head was still bent, but her shoulders shook. A jolt went through him. He'd seen the tears but heard nothing. Her soundless crying shook him.

He put the poker back and slipped his arm back into the other crutch. He hadn't felt awkward in awhile. He did now, but it was nothing compared to whatever had brought her here.

Three steps, and he stopped beside her. "Come sit with me."

She shook her head. "I'm...fine."

"I can't fight you and handle the crutches. Be good. Come on over." He enclosed her hand in his and gave it a gentle tug.

She didn't move. He tugged again, swung around and moved to the couch.

"Alexis?" He slid his arms out of the crutches and set them down beside the sofa. When she glanced at him, he put out his hand.

Slipping off the chair, she walked to the sofa. He reached for her, entwined her fingers with his and pulled her down next to him. She came to rest against the leg that ended in a stump, but he couldn't help that.

His eyes focused on the chair she'd just left. No purse there. *She hadn't brought her gun?* She'd come to talk to him and left her purse with the gun in the car? Was that an oversight or did she trust him?

"They're going to withdraw the complaint."

He brought his mind back. "Who? Jessica and her mom?"

"Yes." Her voice sounded thick.

No wonder she'd come. He slipped an arm around her. "I can't believe Jessica wants to withdraw the complaint. It must be Dawn."

"It is. Jessica is struggling, but…she really wants to do the right thing."

"Is this something that happens often? People withdrawing the complaint?"

"Yes, too often."

"She'll change her mind."

"Maybe."

She leaned into him, her face against his chest. He stilled for a moment, not moving, just looking down at the firelight playing off her hair. Slowly, he tightened his arm and dropped his mouth against the top of her head.

"Alexis?"

She said nothing. The spot under her face felt cool and wet. Her tears soaked his t-shirt. He reached behind her and drew the throw from the back of the couch and wrapped it around them. Her shoulders began to shake.

Lord, tell me what to do.

"If God is so good…" Her voice came muffled and thick, and he strained to understand what she was saying. "Why does he allow this? Over and over?"

Luke stroked her hair. "I wondered the same thing when my foot was blown off, and when Teresa left. Why is this happening, God? I think everyone does when things go wrong. It doesn't mean He's not there. The world we live in has so many problems, so much evil. We choose the good;

not everyone does. At least, we know we have a choice, and we know what to choose."

She lifted her head. The firelight caught her tears, and his heart jerked. He brushed them off with his thumb.

"You were unsure of Dawn from the start, weren't you? I want justice in this, too. More than I've wanted a lot of things. Even if they won't testify, we will."

"This guy deserves to go to jail," Alexis said.

"Agreed. Did she say why?"

"Jessica? She's just doing what her mom wants. Her mom thinks she's lying and believes Leland's version of the story."

"What?" A fire started inside him. "What version? We saw her. We were there. Doesn't her mother know that?"

"She's listening to Leland."

"How can the woman do that?" He fought to control the rising anger. It wouldn't help Alexis. "Doesn't she care about her daughter?"

"She thinks by ignoring it, by aborting the baby, Jessica's life will get back to normal. She has no idea what she's saying. Life is never the same. You can't just wish it away. And aborting the baby? When Jessica believes the way she does? That would add more trauma. There is no easy fix for this. It is a tragedy and must be treated as such, not ignored."

He let the silence hang for a second as he digested her words. "But Dawn was at the hospital with Jessica. Isn't she still angry about what Leland did?"

"She arrived after the rape test. Jessica had cleaned up and put on that pair of scrubs the nurse gave her, remember? Her mother wasn't there to see what she looked like before. And Leland told her Jessica fought him when he locked her in the room. That's why she was beat up."

"The rape test will have his DNA, won't it?"

"Yes, but it takes a while for the results to come."

"Still, it will prove her daughter is telling the truth, prove that the rape happened."

"No, it doesn't prove rape. It only proves they had sex.

They have her deposition, but Jessica's testimony is still critical. It's amazing how much people can ignore when they want to believe a lie." He blew out a breath in frustration. "You tried to convince Jessica, I'm sure. Do you want me to talk with her?"

"You can." She swiped at a tear.

"So, without her testimony...?"

"They'll offer him a plea bargain. Have him plea to a lesser crime or get a lesser sentence." Her voice grated. "It happens more than you think."

"You hate it."

Her eyes rose to search his. "The perpetrator gets off. He's out. To do it again. But often you have to do it to get a conviction, but back in Atlanta, my boss pushed for trial whenever he could."

Luke tightened his arms once more. After a minute, she drew away, leaving cool dampness in place of her warmth.

"I'm sorry." She straightened. "I shouldn't have come. You were asleep."

"Don't apologize. I don't mind."

"I moved here to get away from this. The...the cases, the abuse, the rape. I didn't think I could take anymore, and I'm right in the middle again. I talked with the prosecutor after Jessica and her mom went, but they are much more laid back here than we are in Atlanta. And, of course, they want a solid case to prosecute. I wanted to shake the woman."

He tried to see her face. "Are they more laid back here or more laid back than you want them to be?"

Her eyes focused on his for a moment then dropped. "Every time I prosecuted a case and the defendant got off, it was like it happened all over again."

He stilled. "What happened all over again?"

She didn't answer. The silence lengthened. Finally, she cleared her throat. "If the victim gives testimony, we often have a good case; but too often, the victim bails."

"Like now."

"Yes."

"It's not your fault. You shouldn't take it personally." He moved a thumb across her jaw. "Alexis, it's like what happened all over again?"

Her head dipped. Silence. He waited, watching the fire, praying wordlessly.

"I...I was raped at sixteen."

His insides clenched, and his arm across her shoulders tightened. *He'd known it. Inside, he'd known it.*

"He held a knife to my throat and...and threatened to kill me." Her voice broke. She cleared it again. "Every time one of them gets off, it's like he's getting away with it again. Like they're both getting away with it."

"Both?"

"Yes, I..."

Two men had raped her when she was sixteen, or she'd been raped at sixteen and again later? A fire started inside. Either way, he'd like to get hold of the men for five minutes. Just five minutes. His jaw tightened, but he waited a moment before he spoke. "They never caught them?"

"No. I mean...I..." She stopped.

"Did you know them? What hap—" He hesitated, swallowed, and forced a gentler tone into his next question. "Can you tell me about it?"

Her hesitation was longer. "I can try."

Chapter 12

Alexis' hands tightened on the wheel. The drive to Luke's place felt odd this time. Calling this a date threw her, even if he hadn't said the word. She hadn't either until this morning. When he asked yesterday, between classes, she could tell he had waited for her.

"Come ride," he said. "Mandy and Sandy need the exercise, and so do I. It's great to ride through the trees this time of year, but the leaves are almost gone. They'll be bare soon."

"I don't—"

"You pick the time – morning or afternoon. Don't say no."

Students passed and turned their heads toward them. Everyone would be aware he'd asked her out if she didn't move this along.

"Okay. All right, but I have a few errands in the morning."

He winked at her and turned. "Any time tomorrow is fine." And he disappeared in the opposite direction.

Just exercising the horses, that's all they were doing.

His care the other night, the gentleness that followed his anger and had surprised her. She understood anger against the perpetrators, had felt it many years; but his concern for her touched something deep that she hadn't dealt with yet.

Pulling into the long drive, she remembered the downpour that first night. He had said, "Trust me," and while she had not depended on it, she found out that she could, indeed, trust him. Everything he did, he did with integrity.

She liked his solidness – not just the physical – but the solid way he lived his life. He followed his beliefs. She always admired people who lived what they believed, acted out the main precepts in their lives.

The cool November air rushed around her as she climbed from the Jaguar. She grabbed her jacket from the passenger seat and slipped it on. The sky shimmered with an intense aqua shade, and the huge sassafras tree in front of the big bay window glowed with a thin covering of orange and red leaves. The colors against the sky awed her for a minute.

Such beauty, like when she'd spotted Maximus running along the road. That same wonder filled her now. She understood belief in God on days like these.

The bang, bang, bang of hammering reached her. She listened until it ceased and headed toward the back. Rounding the corner of the house, she saw Luke and stopped.

He held a long section of wooden fencing in front of him. He was shirtless. As he swung the rail toward the fence, the muscles in his arms and across his chest jumped.

"Give me a minute, Alexis."

He'd seen her. So had the dog. Farley ran forward, circled and lifted his head. She patted it, watching Luke as he turned and settled the rail into the notched poles that were ready for it. Muscles bulged across his back.

She wasn't a prude, but, really, couldn't the man wear a shirt? It was cool today.

He straightened, turned her way and gave a welcoming smile. "I'm doing away with the wire fence. When I sit on the deck, I want to see wood. What do you think?"

Think? For a moment, she wondered what he'd asked. She stared at a large tattoo of a cross on the inside of his right arm before looking past him to the rolling land. "You mean about the fence?"

"Yes." He waved at a long section that he'd finished. "What do you think?"

She focused on the fence. "It's nice. I understand what you mean." She shifted her gaze over to the barn then back to the fence. "I like it."

He nodded and smiled and walked her way.

Alexis looked past him again and took a step backward. "Are the horses in the barn?"

"Yes. You're up to a ride, right? I didn't mean to push you yesterday."

"I'm fine. Yes, I'd love to ride." One of the horses whinnied. She turned and headed to the barn.

Luke studied her. Her quick, long steps took her to the building, and she disappeared through the doorway. He frowned.

Except for one glance, she'd looked every place but at him and took off like Farley after a squirrel. What was wrong? He hadn't had time to upset her, but she sure hadn't wanted to look at him. He glanced at the barn, staring at the doorway where she'd disappeared.

She'd acted as if...

He walked over to the fence post, grabbed his t-shirt and pulled it over his head. He didn't need the jacket. The morning had started cool but felt warm as he worked. So, he'd taken his shirt off and dropped it next to his jacket.

Nah. That couldn't be what bothered her. Could it? He felt the beginnings of a grin and swallowed it before heading her way.

She stood at the far end, brushing Mandy. His body blocked some of the sunlight, but she didn't turn around.

"Alexis."

She didn't look at him. "Yeah?"

"You don't have to do that."

"I'm fine. I told you. I use to do this at the stable."

"I brushed them and cleaned their hooves earlier."

He walked over to her, leaned forward and took the brush from her hand. In slow motion, she turned and raised her head. He watched closely. Relief filled her eyes when she looked at him, but her cheeks were flushed.

Putting on the shirt had been a smart move, but he couldn't control his grin this time. "Are you hot?"

Her eyes rounded, and she twisted back to the mare.

He sucked in his breath. *Idiot. What kind of question was that?* The one at the top of his head, but he hadn't meant to say it. "I meant...you look warm. Do you want something to drink?"

"I'm fine." She shoved past him and marched out of the barn.

She was fine all right, but warmth wouldn't flush her cheeks today. It had to be something else. His grin was back. He hadn't meant to embarrass her, but she'd caught him off guard. Better get the horses saddled before she stalked off and went home.

"Alexis." He made his voice rough. "I can't get all three. Come help, will you?"

When she appeared again, he kept his look and tone level. "If you can saddle Mandy, I'll get Sandy and then Max.

"We're taking all three?"

"I'll ride Sandy. You can lead with Mandy." He led Sandy to where the saddles sat on the wall mounts he'd made. He threw a blanket on and straightened it, before settling the saddle on top. "We'll take her out for a while then bring her back, then take a better ride with just Max and Mandy."

"Okay."

"You want a run, too?" He pointed to the other saddle. Blankets sat on top of it. As he moved away, she brought Mandy to the saddle mounts.

"I'd love a good run."

"How long has it been since you've ridden?"

"You don't need to worry about it."

"No?" He glanced back and looked her up and down. "You'll be sore tomorrow."

"I might be, but you won't know it."

She forced Mandy past him. He had to shove Sandy back a step or two to give her room. Now that sounded like some sort of challenge. *Was she flirting with him? Nah.* He was sure Alexis Jergenson didn't flirt. Of course, until a few minutes ago, he hadn't thought that his shirtlessness would bother her, either.

"Is that how you win cases?" he asked, following her out. They both stopped to fasten the cinches. "Intimidation?"

"Whatever it takes."

He laughed. "I'd like to see you in the courtroom one day."

She turned. A smile appeared. "Maybe you'll get the chance."

He lifted a brow. Was she thinking of practicing in Tennessee? "That would be nice."

Her eyes reflected her smile. She'd relaxed again, and he liked what it did to her. He reached up and gently tugged a long piece of that shiny hair. Her mouth opened, and he dropped his gaze to it. Keeping one hand on Sandy's lead, he slipped an arm around her waist and pulled her forward. His mouth was an inch from hers when the change in her stance and her eyes stopped him.

He drew back four inches, keeping his focus on eyes now dark with fright. At least he knew the problem this time. He could deal with this if she'd let him.

"I'm going to kiss you."

She started to pull away, but his arm tightened. Her eyes rounded, and he forced his arm to loosen.

"I'm going to kiss you. Nothing else." He let his eyes drop to her mouth again. "Just kiss you."

He touched her mouth with his. She stood rigid against his arm, her mouth as stiff as her back. Not what he'd expected, but he hadn't thought ahead. She'd been raped twice, and had not gone out with anyone since that jerk of a boyfriend promised to stop when she asked. And hadn't.

The awkwardness in her stance, in her face, touched him. He drew a breath, dropped his arm, and touched her face. "Let's try that again."

She shook her head but didn't move. He sensed her wavering – to run or to stay.

"I won't hold you this time. Relax."

He leaned in, moving slow, like a clam his grandmother would say. She held herself rigid. His mouth caressed hers, and he turned his head, moving his lips across hers. He was about to draw away, when her mouth offered an awkward response. Heat shot to his toes, and it took everything in him to stay still. He wanted her in his arms, wanted to hold her tight and hard against him. His hands clenched. The blood raced to his head, and he hauled himself away.

They stared at each other, both inhaling deep breaths.

His smile felt lopsided. "Not as bad as you thought?"

Apprehension still edged her eyes, but she shook her head. He lifted a hand to her cheek and drew his fingers along her jaw.

"Trust me, Alexis. I won't hurt you. I like you. Kissing is just a way of expressing that."

A flush crept up her throat and into her cheeks. "I know that."

He laughed, leaned forward to steal another quick kiss and grabbed her hand. "Come on then. Let's take a ride."

Alexis let herself sink deeper into the hot water and let the tub's geysers ease her aching muscles. She *was* sore. Tomorrow promised a long day of stiffness, but she'd work off some of it in the morning before leaving for work.

She liked to ride, liked the feel of the horse beneath her, the smell of leather, the freedom of going places you didn't get to go on foot or car. Years had passed, but it all came back. After Luke changed horses, they explored his property, crossed the road and then raced through the level fields.

She touched her lips and thought of the kiss. *No, two kisses. Three?* She'd dated a few times during college, but her fear rested too close to the surface, and the men's hormones did, too. It never worked. And then at law school, Brock had taken his time, patiently befriending and encouraging her. Until that night…

She shuddered and closed her eyes.

Even though she'd gone willingly to the cabin, Luke said it was not her fault, as John had, not to blame herself. She had been upfront and honest with Brock.

Luke's anger at the man touched her. Until last week, she'd never told anyone but John about the second rape. She was used to her brother's protectiveness, had felt it from the time she was small, but especially after the first rape. Luke's response had differed from John's. She couldn't exactly describe it, but having him hear and understand what she'd been through helped ease the long-hidden pain and the violation somehow.

She rested the back of her head against the folded towel on the porcelain tub and thought of that. Luke was different. She couldn't quite nail down what it was. *Trustworthy.* She hesitated. Was Luke trustworthy? Maybe she assumed he was. Like Brock. No. No, Luke had never taken advantage, and he could have.

His character – intelligent, hard-working, with a willingness to come to another person's rescue – was admirable. She thought of Jessica. Luke hadn't argued or backed down. Instead, he did what was needed at the time. And he'd been there for her, too. That aspect of his personality, she prized – to rescue someone, to save someone who needed it.

Her domestic violence cases were filled with women and children, even men, who needed to be rescued. Life had battered them, then people did the same.

The word "saved" echoed in her mind. Was she getting religious? Or was it just her mind picking up the strands of Luke's teachings, or the things she'd heard from the students, or from the Chapel services?

Jesus saves. Redeems. Gives new life. All things she'd heard repeatedly since coming to the college.

She stood and grabbed a towel, wrapping it around her. She needed to tell Luke she wasn't a Christian. It was time.

For her not to say something now would be deceptive, but maybe she'd read a few chapters in her Bible tonight. She could at least tell him she was doing that to help smooth over the fact that she hadn't told him before.

And maybe, just maybe, she'd read something to help her understand about that new life to which he referred.

Chapter 13

The warmth inside him contrasted with the cold outside. They stood in the college parking lot next to her Jaguar, both bundled up against the frosty weather. The leaves had disappeared from most trees, and their skeletal outlines stood in black relief against the silvered sky.

"Thank you for dinner, Luke. I enjoyed the company and the food."

He ran a finger down her jaw line, feeling his smile widen. "Then it was worth the time it took me to talk you into it."

During dinner, his hormones had kicked into an excess of activity – her mouth, her hair, the way she laughed – all of it caused havoc with his good intentions. He slipped his hand under her hair to the back of her neck.

"Alexis." He heard the roughness in his voice and cleared his throat.

Her half-opened mouth reflected her nervousness, and he straightened, took a deep breath, and sought for a diversion.

"Do you know if you're going to continue teaching or perhaps go back into law?"

She hesitated, frowning, and shivered against the wind. Good enough reason to pull her into his arms. She came, uncertainly.

"I have thought about practicing again. I...I just don't know."

"What made you give up law and move here?" When she said nothing, he tilted his head to see her better. "Prosecuting cases like Jessica's could cause burnout. You said that the other night. Is that what happened?"

She shrugged. "That was part of it."

"Your work in Atlanta with the rape crisis center and that house you established for victims of violence. Couldn't you duplicate that here, with or without going back into practice?"

Her brows lifted. "Perhaps. I hadn't thought of it."

"I have." He cleared his throat again, drew his focus from her mouth again. "Sorry. If I'm being too inquisitive, tell me."

"No. I don't mind telling *you*."

The huskiness of her voice and her look was tinder to the fire he kept trying to control. He wanted to kiss her mouth, her eyes, the place at the back of her neck where her hair fell like silk.

He slid his hands up and down her back and bent his head, covering her mouth with his. His arms tightened, and he savored the feeling of holding her. After a moment, she leaned against him, her mouth softening. A wave of response hit him, and his pulse beat hard against the side of his head. He forced himself to push back and away from her. The woman had no idea what she did to him. He allowed the cool air to rush between them, needing it.

"That was good. Thank you." She put hand to her mouth. "I mean…the dinner."

He caught her hand, feeling his grin. She hadn't meant to thank him for the kiss. "It *was* good." He laughed when she turned her head away, squeezed her then became serious. "I can be patient, Alexis. I don't mind, but I would like to see where this relationship might go. Are you willing to do that?"

"Yes, but I… I…" She stopped.

"What?"

"I need to tell you something."

"All right."

"I…" She removed her hand from his and took a short step back. "I'm not a Christian."

He wasn't sure he'd heard right. "What?"

"I'm not a Christian."

"You're not?"

"No."

Things went silent around them. His heart stopped, skipped. "That's...impossible." *It was, wasn't it? Impossible. Of all the problems they might have, being "unequally yoked" had never surfaced.* "You're teaching here. They only hire Christians."

"I know. I..." The strength in her face appeared to melt. "I..."

He felt sick. *What was she saying?* "You lied on the application?"

"No, I..." Her voice sounded ragged. "I told them, but they were desperate; and...and I was, too. Neither the Dean or I felt right about it, but he said not to say anything. Everyone would assume..."

He didn't care about the details. Only one thing mattered. "You're not a Christian?"

"No. The President knows, of course. He and Cliff. No one else."

His mind flew over the ramifications. Seeing where the relationship would go? Useless. He could not marry her, would not. And that was where he'd hoped the relationship would go, whether he'd let himself think it or not. But now... Balls of steel rolled inside him, slicing open the places of pain and betrayal he thought were healed.

"Sharee told me about the opening. Called me from Indonesia, in fact. She said they might not hire me, but to apply." She stopped for a moment. "I never meant to deceive you."

He shook his head, the pain inside changing, igniting embers. "You not only deceived me, but every student you've taught, all the professors, the other staff members. I can't believe the President allowed this."

She swallowed. "Does it mean that much?"

"Does it mean that much?" He drew back. "Haven't you

heard anything while you've been here? Do you just turn it off – the talk about God, about Jesus?"

She flinched at his words. He sounded harsh even to himself. *Lord, don't let me hurt her like I'm hurting. Don't let me lash out.*

"Alexis, everything we're about here has to do with God – His love, His leading. Our lives are dedicated to Him. That is what a Bible college is. Have you heard nothing at all?"

"Yes, I've heard." Her voice jumped an octave. "I know you're all serious, but none of it makes sense. A God who created the world. Jesus, the savior. It's not logical. There's no evidence—"

"The evidence is there if you look for it."

She shook her head.

The enemy had worked overtime in her. He'd never seen it, never guessed. A cavern of huge proportions existed between them. The flames grew inside him.

"You have four eye witnesses."

She frowned. "What? Who?"

"The Gospels. Matthew, Mark, Luke and John."

Her frown deepened. "If they lived, and if they can be believed."

"You believe Plato, don't you? And Aristotle? Their writings."

"Yes, but…"

"The writings of the Old and New Testament are no different than many other writings at that time. We take those others at face value. The only reason you wouldn't take these the same way is because of a predisposition to disbelieve them." He took a deep breath. "Truth has stared you in the face all these weeks, and you haven't seen it. I can't make you believe, but I wish I could."

He had tried to keep his voice level but the shock of what she'd revealed stunned him. *Walk away. Before you do or say something you will regret.* He turned.

She caught his arm. "Luke. You're the only man I've

trusted in years. Don't just walk off."

He heard the hurt in her voice. Her pain multiplied his. "I appreciate that...honor. And it is an honor. But there are many decent men out there. We're not all rapists. Find a respectable one, one that will walk you up the aisle."

Her eyes widened. "Don't leave like this."

He slipped his arm free from her hold. "I have to. I need to get my head on straight."

"No one, but John, has it on straighter."

He forced a half-smile, turned again, and stepped to his truck. Her eyes singed his back. When he climbed into the truck and started the engine, he looked at her again. She stood there, arms crossed, clutching her shoulders, alone.

He loved her. He knew it now, and he knew something else. The picture of her standing there, alone, would stay with him a long time.

&

The phone chimed on her way home. Alexis snatched it from the passenger seat and stared at the number on the screen. Tears starred the readout. She blinked her eyes and looked again. Her heart thudded, and her shoulders slumped.

Jessica.

She dropped the phone back on the seat. It chimed again. She didn't want to talk. Not to anyone. The phone's ring came once more. Alexis sighed and raised it to her ear.

"Yes?"

"Professor Jergenson?"

Alexis cleared her throat. "Jessica, I told you to call me Alexis. You were living at my house. Call me Alexis."

"I know. It's just...well, hard."

"That's okay. What's up?"

"Are you okay? You sound funny."

Alexis stared at the car lights flashing past. Was she okay? No. Would she be okay? Yeah, someday. "I'm fine, Jessica. A cold, I have a cold." Lying could become a new part of her life. "What is it?"

"Can…can I come to stay again? Tonight?"

The Jag swerved. Alexis wrestled it back into the middle of the lane. A headline flashed across her mind. *Appalachian College Professor Dead in Freak Accident.* And Luke would never forgive himself. He'd think he caused it. She needed to drive more carefully. She could not put that on Luke's shoulders, no matter how angry he was with her.

"Profess— Alexis?" Jessica's voice drew her back.

Alexis sighed. "That's fine. You're coming tonight?"

"Yes."

"Tell me why you're coming. Did you and your mom have a fight?"

"No, I…"

"Jessica, if you come to stay with me, you'll have to tell her where you are. Don't let her worry."

"I won't, but I'll call her after I get there. I haven't told her yet that I changed my mind."

"About what?"

"About testifying. You were right, and the people at the pregnancy center, and Professor Stephens."

"You talked with Luke?" The jump and sputter of her heart hurt.

"Yes. He…he said a lot of the same things you said. And then he asked me to pray."

"And?"

"And God said the same thing, too."

"He did?"

"Yeah. I mean…of course, I didn't hear this audible voice, but when I woke up this morning, I knew. I knew I had to testify."

❧

Luke strode across the lobby toward the President's office. He'd been summoned. Good. Because his plans for the day included a conference with the President and with the Dean, whether they wanted it or not.

He hadn't seen or overheard Alexis this morning – better for both of them. Maybe this summons had something to do with it. No matter. The President would hear what he thought about their little plan and hear it soon.

When he reached the office, the President's administrative assistant waved him through. He opened the door and stepped inside.

President Jim Edwards sat behind his desk. It looked as if he'd run his fingers through his silver hair numerous times. He nodded at Luke and opened his mouth to say something, but from his right, Dawn Saltare jumped to her feet and pointed in Luke's direction.

"You stay away from Jessica!" Her voice shrilled. "He and that other Professor – that woman – are interfering in my daughter's life. They're telling her to do things that I don't want her to do."

Luke lifted his eyebrows, glanced at the President and back to Dawn. "Jessica is over eighteen, an adult. She can talk to whomever and do whatever she wants."

"I thought it was funny that you two were so concerned about her. And that other professor let us stay with her. Who would do that for people they don't know?"

"Alexis was concerned about Jessica's safety. And yours."

"I think she just wanted a case. I know she's a lawyer. She's just drumming up business."

Luke frowned. "Who told you that?"

"That's none of your business. It's true, isn't it?" She whirled on the President. "You see what I mean? These two are messing in people's lives, and it better stop. Because if it doesn't, this college is going to find its name in the evening news; and it's not going to be pretty!"

Jim looked over his glasses at Luke. "Can you expand on this?"

"I can tell you that Jessica talked with me, and after I heard her story, I took her to talk with Alexis." He hesitated.

"She'd been abused by her mother's boyfriend."

"So she says! I—"

"Mrs. Saltare, please let Professor Stephens finish."

Luke crossed his arms over his chest. "As you know, Alexis has handled abuse cases in Georgia and has established a house for victims of abuse."

"My daughter—"

"Mrs. Saltare, please."

"However, Alexis cannot practice law in Tennessee. She is only trying to help Jessica."

"Well, I want Jessica out of her place today!" Dawn's voice rose.

Luke uncrossed his arms and leaned forward. "I thought you both went home the other day."

"We did, but Jessica went back last night."

"Did she?" Luke shifted his gaze to the President again. "I think Alexis could clear this up."

Jim nodded. "Probably, but she isn't here today. She called in and said she would be out today for personal reasons."

"Personal reasons that have to do with my daughter!"

Luke stared past her. Alexis hadn't come for class? Well, he could understand – after yesterday. And then if Jessica did show up at her door last night... His chest emptied, leaving a crater inside. Last night he'd alternated between pacing and wanting to throw something to sitting and staring at the fire. He had stoked it so much that he had to open all the windows to rid the house of the extra heat. Today, he stoked his anger and held onto it to stave off the other emotions churning inside, but somehow, the thought that she wasn't in the building left an even greater abyss.

"Luke?" The President's voice reached him.

He shifted. "Yes?"

"I think you and I and Professor Jergenson should talk about this on Monday."

"Monday?" Dawn's voice shrilled again. "I want something done today."

The President stepped from behind his desk. "Now, Mrs. Saltare, I can't do anything until I've talked with Professor Jergenson and your daughter. Jessica is an adult as Professor Stephens pointed out. I will have to hear what she says about this." He walked to the door and opened it.

"Well, she's not thinking clearly, and she's acting out." Her eyes narrowed at Luke. "Too many people are trying to influence her."

"Come out here, Mrs. Saltare, and give my assistant your name and address. I will call you as soon as I speak to your daughter." He led her through the doorway and closed it behind them.

Luke stared at the closed door. Last time he spoke with Dawn, she said he and Alexis were angels from heaven. Things had changed when she and Jessica moved from Alexis' condo, but what was going on? He reached for his phone before his brain stopped him.

He couldn't call Alexis even if she would take his call. The emptiness in his chest returned, and, with it, the anger.

He stepped to the President's desk and punched Cliff's extension.

"Dean Smithfield. Can I help you?"

Luke's jaw tightened. "Yes. I need to see you in the President's office as soon as you can get here."

"Luke?"

"Yes."

"I'm on my way."

"Good."

He cradled the phone. In a moment, Jim returned. He moved around Luke and sat in his chair. Neither said anything.

Jim's fingers rapped on the polished wood of his desk. "I'll need some more information before I talk with her daughter."

Luke nodded, picked up a picture from the President's desk and stared at the family portrait. *How could this man whom he so respected do something unethical and secretive?*

He lifted his head.

"I need something from you, too. I need more information on why Alexis Jergenson was hired and told to keep secret the fact that she is not a Christian."

"What?"

"You heard me."

"I heard you, but I don't know what you're talking about."

"Alexis told me about this...this little scheme yesterday. It was not a good conversation for either of us. She specifically said you and Cliff knew she wasn't a Christian and hired her. She said—"

The door opened. The academic dean stepped in and closed it behind him. "Luke, your voice carries when you're upset."

Luke's jaw tightened. "I'm not trying to keep any of this under wraps."

Cliff nodded and stepped forward. "I thought when you called just now that you had to know about Alexis. I'm sorry. I understand your anger. I had no idea you and she would become involved. It never entered my mind that something like this would happen. And Jim knew nothing about it."

The President pushed up from his chair. "What didn't I know?"

"That I hired Alexis knowing she wasn't a Christian." Cliff held up a hand. "I know our policy, but I decided to make this a special case. I did not tell you because I wasn't sure if you would agree. I told Alexis, however, that you knew. I lied. Christian or not, she would not have come without your approval and the Board's. Her integrity is high. I finessed her into coming. We were desperate, and so was she."

Desperate. The word reverberated in Luke's mind. Desperate to get away from the cases that kept her own wounds open. Desperate enough to run to a small Christian college and pretend she was something she wasn't. And he'd brought Jessica to her and scraped the wounds open again.

And yesterday? What had he done to her yesterday? He

hadn't handled it correctly. His record with her was not just poor, it was appalling. Not that the outcome could be any different, no matter how he'd handled it.

He glared at the Dean. "What you did was deceptive and detrimental to the college."

"What I did was for the college."

"Deception, going against policy, will not help the college in the long run. You think God will reward that?"

"From what I've heard, Alexis is an excellent teacher. The students are thrilled with her classes."

"That has nothing to do with—"

The President dropped a book onto his desk. Both men's heads jerked his way. His eyes focused on the Dean. "Cliff, you and I have some things to discuss. Luke, give us the time. Please wait on me before you spread this around."

"I'll wait, but I won't let this get swept under the rug."

"No one's asking you to."

Luke nodded, glared again at the Dean, and walked out the door.

Chapter 14

The sound of the truck engine reached him before it rounded the corner of the house and pulled to a halt near the barn. Luke glanced at the tack in his hands. His Saturday routine could wait. He'd half expected a visit.

Her brother climbed from the truck, shut the door, and stood glaring at him. Yeah. He'd guessed this missionary pilot had a temper that he fought to control as much as Luke did his. *We all have our foibles, a thorn in the flesh with which to contend, don't we, Lord?*

John Jergenson's face and clenched fists displayed his battle. After a few moments, the man's hands relaxed.

"Luke."

Luke nodded. "John."

Silence stood between them for a moment.

"You might as well have raped her." John's anger, though under control, was still there.

A similar rage shot through Luke. He stepped forward, but stopped. The man loved his sister. They'd been through a lot this year. Let him say what he wanted and get the pain out.

John's eyes narrowed. "She trusted you."

"I trusted her. She lied to me, to her students."

"She didn't lie. If you'd asked her, she would have told you the truth. The Dean instructed her not to say anything. You assumed—"

"He was wrong."

"Yes, he was wrong. I didn't know what she was asked to do. Sharee didn't know. We would have advised her differently. But Alexis is *not* a Christian. She didn't see this as a big deal."

"So she said. It is."

"Of course it is, especially if you're in love with her."

Luke tightened his jaw, turned to the gate and flipped the halter and lead over the post. He took his time. John said nothing.

Luke looked back at him. "Whether I am or not, it doesn't make any difference now."

"Of course, it does. It makes all the difference. It's why you would walk away. You can't marry her if she's not a Christian. Otherwise, you would have told her what she did was wrong, explained why it was wrong and tried to help her make it right. But you didn't. You ran."

Luke's chin jutted. His body stiffened. He'd wanted to hit something or somebody these last two days. Maybe he'd get the chance now.

John raised a brow. "Well, come on. Give it a shot." But a smile tugged at the corners of his mouth. "We'd both feel better, but I doubt it's what the Lord wants."

Luke scowled.

John moved forward. "Look, if this was anyone else, you'd at least try to explain why you felt what she did was wrong. Give her some grace."

Luke glared.

"Or you could witness to her, give her a chance to receive Jesus as her Savior."

"She's been in my class. She's heard what I have to say."

"Teaching a class is not a direct witness."

"It never works between people who are close. It's just me shoving my religion down her throat."

"How would you know unless you tried?"

"You've tried, haven't you?"

"Of course, but I'm not giving up. If you give up, just dump her like she's not worth the bother, then you've done the same thing those other men did – prove to her that she's not worth anything. You've got to get past your hurt and your anger and think of her."

"I have thought of her. Too much." He swept a hand toward the barn and the house. "Over the last few weeks, thought of her here with me. I assumed the leg would be a problem, not this."

"So cope with it. Give her a chance. And if it doesn't work...well, give her the full explanation not the abbreviated one you did the other day."

Give her a chance. Yeah. And tear both their hearts apart.

"At least pray about it."

He clenched his fists and stared at the other man. John stared back. Silence reigned until Luke nodded his assent. He knew before praying that her brother was right, and, deep inside, a tiny ember of hope burned.

Fool, he told himself; but that didn't stop the slight uptick in his heart.

෴

Alexis considered the long tumultuous weekend that had passed. She couldn't leave Jessica yet. She palmed her phone and made the necessary call. She'd be out one more day. Missing class both Friday and today would be hard on her students and herself, but right now, leaving Jessica and facing Luke were two mountains she couldn't – or wouldn't – climb.

She rested her elbows on the kitchen table and looked over her cup as Jessica walked into the kitchen.

The girl had broken down as soon as she crossed the threshold Thursday night. Vacillating between sobs and anger, Jessica's "What ifs" and "Why me?" echoed those of Alexis at sixteen. She could only hold the girl and listen.

Jessica's struggles had triggered memories in Alexis, memories of the first rape and then the second. Her parents had insisted she report the rape at sixteen, but she had never reported the second assault, never told anyone but John; and she'd sworn him to secrecy. Then she'd told Luke. Feeling her heart jerk at that thought, she swallowed against the tightening of her throat and sighed.

Why had she believed Brock? She'd wanted to, wanted to believe that she could be free again. She'd let him talk her into the fact that in order to get over the first rape, she needed to have sex with someone who cared. In being so naive, she had invited her own violation. She had gone freely with him that weekend. So, the rape had been her fault. At least, that's what she'd thought. Both John and Luke vehemently disagreed. She had told Brock "no" once they arrived at the cabin, and "no was no" both men insisted. Date rape might not have the same stigma to some, but it was the same act, tearing through dignity, trust, and personal confidence. And she was not to blame.

Alexis' fingers tightened around her cup. She bowed her head and took a sip of the cocoa-colored liquid. Should she share with Jessica what had happened to her? Would it help or hinder things?

The girl's anger and heartache were complicated by her feelings of betrayal from her mother and heightened by the fact that Leland had not been arrested. What if he found her again? Fear, Alexis knew, would follow her for some time. The multitude of emotions flowing through her needed validation, and Alexis shared the knowledge she'd accumulated from the rape crisis center and from victims she'd represented over the years.

She'd always held herself aloof when being told of the trauma women and children—even some men—went through from assaults. But now, as she ministered to Jessica, the words she used chipped away at her own hardness. Telling Luke had cracked that rigidity, and the openings had widened as the weekend progressed. The desire to be free of the past seemed like a mythical siren calling her. Could she ever be free?

Alexis covered a yawn, shoved the personal thoughts aside and studied Jessica. Something was different this morning.

The girl had combed her hair, washed her face, and put on make-up. Not something she'd done either Saturday or Sunday.

Jessica brought her coffee to the table and sat across from Alexis. "I need to forgive Leland and my mom."

Alexis straightened. Where had that come from?

"Rachel called last night. I...we talked for a long time. No matter what either of them has done to me, I need to forgive them."

Forgive them? Alexis didn't want to go there. Wanting to be free of the emotions that bound her did not equate to forgiving the offender. Did it?

She changed the subject. "So, your mother still wants you to withdraw the complaint?"

Jessica glanced down, then met her gaze. "Yes."

Alexis nodded and sipped at the warm liquid in her cup. More cream and a quarter bar of chocolate in the coffee would help. She put it down. "But you won't withdraw it, and you'll give evidence at the trial?"

"Yes. To both." Jessica lowered the mug she held. "Professor Jergenson, forgiving him doesn't mean that what he did was right. It means I release him from my own vengeance. I give him to God. God, after all, forgave us our sins. That doesn't mean we don't have consequences in this life. In this world, there are often consequences. Leland will have to live with his, but I...I have to do what is right."

Okay, they weren't going to get past this. "You forgive him?"

"Well, I'm working on it. I'm willing. Rachel helped me see that last night. I have to forgive."

"You have to?"

"The same way I have to have the baby. Because God says we must, *and*," she emphasized the conjunction, "He will bless it if I do. Sometimes, we can't see the far-reaching effects of something, but God does. He's all-knowing. I know He will work things out for the good. I...I just got off-kilter for a while. Mom is not a believer. She doesn't understand."

Alexis turned her head away. The force that had driven her life came from anger not forgiveness. She'd wanted justice all these years. She still did.

"You know, Jessica, I'm not as big on forgiveness as you are."

"I figured that, Professor Jergenson. In fact, a number of us wondered if you really knew Jesus."

"Why do you say that?"

"You never reference God in the classroom. You let others talk about Him, but you don't."

Alexis studied her coffee for a minute. It's not like it wouldn't get out. She'd be gone in a few weeks, anyway, if not sooner. Being on the same campus with Luke, the same floor, listening to his voice coming down the hall from his classroom... Her heart stalled. She had never imagined caring this much.

In other circumstances, she'd finish what she started; but once everyone knew, they might ask her to leave, anyway. Luke would probably talk with the Dean, and even if he didn't, she would. The charade had lasted too long.

"So you all decided I wasn't a Christian?"

"Pretty much." Jessica took a sip of the dark liquid in her mug, added more vanilla flavoring and smiled. "It's all right, though. We all like you and your class."

Alexis smiled. Warmth stirred inside. "Thank you for saying that."

"We've learned so much. About the law, about people, and how that all connects to God whether you formally taught it or not."

"How it all connects to God?"

"Yes. You know, if you stay within the laws of this country, for the most part, you stay out of trouble. I mean the laws are meant to help people. We get it that they don't always. But they're man's laws. God's laws are different.

He's perfect, so they are, too. If we stay within His laws, then our lives are blessed. Now, I'm not saying nothing bad ever happens. That's crazy. We're still in a fight with the devil and sin, but God's blessings come when we do what we know is right."

Alexis sucked in her breath. Her chest hurt. Stay within God's laws. That's what Luke would do. He wouldn't marry her. But he'd thought about it. Find a man, he'd said, that would walk her up the aisle. If he hadn't considered it himself, the words would never have come from his mouth.

Funny. She hadn't thought about marriage in years. Marriage, children, a home. And now, before the desire had fully formed, the dream was snatched from her.

She blinked her eyes. Time for another subject change. "Have you thought more about whether you will raise your baby yourself or place him for adoption?"

Jessica shook her head then smiled. "Him or her."

Alexis smiled, too. "Yes, him or her. When will you find out?"

"In a few more weeks. They have free sonograms at the pregnancy center. I can probably see the heartbeat now. I just need to get down there."

""Will that make a difference to you?"

"Oh, no. I just want him or her to be healthy and happy."

"You'll need to make a doctor's appointment soon. But you don't have to make a decision about adoption right away." She leaned forward. "Jessica, either decision is a good one."

"I know. I actually picked up some information on adoption the other day."

"Did you?" When Jessica nodded, Alexis examined her. Her talk with Rachel last night had done more than the whole three days of Alexis' "crisis" help. "Tell me about this forgiveness stuff."

"It's what God says we need to do. After all, He forgave us. We talked about the consequences of sin for Leland, but we also have consequences for our own sins, even though they're not as bad as Leland's. It's justice. God is a righteous judge. Funny how we want people to pay for the bad things they do, but we don't think we should have to pay ourselves. Yet, in reality, someone has to pay. Jesus paid the price that we should have paid. He died."

"He died, but we still die."

"Yes, he died physically, and we will, too; but he rose from the grave and lives forever in heaven. Eternal life, Professor Jergenson. Because of his sacrifice, our sins are forgiven; and we will live forever, too."

Alexis shook her head. "That's the part I don't understand. How could a good God let his son die for others?"

"Simple. Jesus wanted to. They formed this plan before the world began."

"Luke mentioned that."

"And Jesus couldn't bear to watch us suffer. We are his bride, you know. He loves us, kind of like you and Professor Stephens."

Her cup went down again. "What?"

"You have the hots for him, don't you?"

Warmth rose in Alexis' cheeks. "I don't know if I would describe it that way, but I like him a lot. Yes."

"I thought so."

"Not that it matters. Now."

"Because you're not a Christian?"

"Yes."

"It's easy to become a Christian. It's just like I said. Jesus paid the price for your sin. All you have to do is believe it and accept it."

Her gaze met Jessica's. "Despite what it looks like, I don't tell people I believe something I don't."

"You can think about it. You can ask God to show you the truth."

Alexis wanted to end the conversation, but she had one more objection. "I don't understand how a good God allows so much evil in the world."

"Everybody has the same question. If there were no evil, how would we know to choose the good? God says he put before us life and death, blessing and cursing; and he asks us to choose the one we want. Then he gives us a big hint, and says 'Choose life.'" Jessica's voice rose. "Look at it this way. You're choosing sides. Which side do you want to be on? God's or Satan's?"

Alexis pushed up from her chair and walked to the sink. The cup and saucer went into it. Jessica came next to her and placed her mug in the sink, also.

"Just think about it, Professor Jergenson. Think and pray and ask God to show you. Give Him a chance."

After a moment's hesitation, Alexis turned from the sink and gave a weak smile. "I'll try, Jessica. That's all I can say. I'll try."

Bang! Bang!

"What in the world?" Alexis turned toward the entryway.

"I bet it's Mom." Jessica ran toward the front. "I knew she'd come to her senses."

Alexis followed her into the hall. "Well, look through the peephole—"

Jessica flung open the door. Leland stood there, a smirk on his face, gun in hand. Jessica's scream ripped from her mouth. He thrust her back into the room and closed the door.

Chapter 15

Alexis hadn't come to work again. Her office door was locked, the lights out. Luke's heart did a double-time beat inside his chest. He should have gone to her condo yesterday after John left. He'd waited. Why? The man was right. Luke couldn't leave things like they were. He pulled his phone from his pocket and punched in her number. No answer.

He had a class in twenty minutes. What would he say to her in that amount of time, anyway? He needed to see her in person.

Rising from the high-backed chair at his desk, he walked to his office window and looked over the parking lot, remembering the jerk in his chest the time he saw Alexis throw herself into John's arms. Then the other feeling when he'd found out John was her brother.

Past the parking lot, the trees edging the grass stood silent and bare, their leaves scattered and gone. Their emptiness echoed in his heart. Another picture of Alexis rose – when she'd jumped into view at the soccer game. His chest tightened. How important she'd become in his life. He'd fought it, but nothing could stop what happened. The third picture differed from the others. In this one, her eyes reflected anger and pain after finding Jessica in the trailer.

The woman had seen much in her life, had been through much. So different from Teresa. And yet…

The marriage had been good for a while. Looking back, he realized that they had married for lust more than love. They were both Christians, and instead of having sex before marriage like so many, they'd waited. After all, he had talked Christianity all his life and believed in God. But they should have sought the Lord's will before marrying. His mom had cautioned him, but he'd wanted his own way.

Teresa had argued with him about joining the army. She hadn't agreed, but once he saw the others coming home, once he heard their stories, nothing could alter his thirst to join. His own stubbornness again.

The war had changed him even before the bomb hit. With life and death so close, when it resides within your hands, you have another view of reality. Then when he came home maimed, she'd hated it, hated what the war had done to him and to them. Her affair was a way to get back at him. They had cared for each other, but neither had the maturity to hold the marriage together, to make it work. She had remarried soon after the divorce – to one of her buff workout buddies.

Luke inhaled past the twinge in his chest. He'd never really forgiven her. He thought he had, but when he saw Alexis that first time, looking so much like her, his anger burst from its hidden place in his heart. He stared past the mountains at the cobalt sky.

Why had he never tried to understand what his leaving and his injury had done to Teresa? All he thought about back then was himself, coping with the injury, hurrying to get back to "normal" as fast as he could. He hadn't seen her pain, he hadn't listened to her—before or after.

Did you direct me, God, or did I go on my own? You're telling me something. Was my timing off? Open my heart to hear what you're saying. Pressure seemed to come from every side.

Whether the timing was off or not, you could still have made it work if we'd listened, if we'd wanted it. Is that what you're saying? Was I too hurt, too prideful after I found out about the affair?

He ran a hand through his hair and stepped back from the window. *The divorce was my fault as much as Teresa's.*

That's what you're saying. I've blamed her entirely. Forgive me, and help her to forgive me. Help me to forgive her.

I've wanted another relationship, and I haven't seen the truth in the first one. John had it right. I have to get my mind off myself.

After a moment, he sighed. And maybe he'd have to put Cliff and that whole business into God's hands, too.

His mind jumped to Alexis. John was right, again. He had run. He hadn't stayed long enough to hear Alexis out. He couldn't do to her what he'd done to Teresa – not hear her. He turned back to the desk, eyed his phone. It wouldn't change the fact that the relationship could not continue, but maybe it would do something else – show her that she was of value, in his sight and in God's.

The impatience hit again. He needed to see her. He picked up the phone and punched in her number once more. When she didn't answer, he shoved his papers into his backpack, wrote a note for the receptionist, and headed out. He'd miss his class, as his note indicated; but Alexis took priority right now.

He couldn't blame her for not answering, but he'd try her phone once again when he got to her condo. Whatever, he wasn't leaving until they talked. When he climbed into the truck, he pulled open the glove box and tore through the papers inside. Hadn't she written her address down for him the last time they'd gone out? He'd asked for it at dinner. He went through the papers again. Nothing.

Where would he have put it? He pulled his wallet out and flipped through it. Again nothing.

The name of her condo? She'd mentioned it, but it hadn't rung a bell. He ran a hand down his face. What was it? He'd get in touch with her brother. No. He had no idea how to do that. What friends did she have at the college? Anyone? She'd kept to herself a lot. It felt like he had searched Google and come up with nothing.

Who would have her address?

Jessica.

He hit the contacts button and flipped through the names, but she didn't answer.

Who else? Someone had to have her address.

The office.

He called the main line.

"Hello, Appalachian Christian College. May I help you?"

"Rachel? Can you get me Professor Jergenson's address?"

"Her address? She's not coming in today. She called earlier and left a message."

"I know she's not there. I need her address. Can you get it for me?"

"You could just call her."

"Rachel." He said the name through gritted teeth.

"Oh, sure. Just a minute."

What would he say to her? Would she listen?

Lord, open her heart. Lead me in all I say and do over the next few hours. Don't let me do anything that will hurt her. Don't let her get hurt. Protect her. Protect Jessica, too.

He frowned. Where had that come from? He drummed on the steering wheel.

"Professor Stephens?"

"Yes?"

"I've got her address."

"Okay. Wait a second. I'll punch it into my GPS as you give it to me."

Alexis watched as Leland continued to pace and rant. He'd accused her of being the main problem in his life. She had called the police; she had talked Jessica into prosecuting. If Alexis had never entered the picture, there'd be no cops chasing him.

The man's wild-eyed look unnerved her, and his hand shook as he held the revolver. The rock in her stomach anchored her to the floor. She had to think, to move. She'd left her purse in the bedroom. If she and Jessica could get there, lock the door, even for a minute... She sat forward on the couch and tried to catch Jessica's eye, but the girl's head was down.

Leland jerked the pistol in her direction. "Don't move, honey. You've caused all the trouble you're going to."

"You're the cause of your own trouble."

His mouth thinned. "Well, we need some attitude adjustment here."

His grin caused a nauseous churn in her stomach.

"And I'm just the one who can do it, aren't I, Jessie?"

Jessica's head rose. "Leave her alone, Leland. She...She hasn't done anything to you."

The man stepped forward as if to hit her, but Alexis threw herself in front of the girl.

"Don't touch her!"

Leland stopped, and the grin returned. "Oh, you two are the rah-rah sisters, is that it? Gonna protect each other from big, bad Leland?" His face changed, and his voice threatened. "Nobody's getting out of here until I get what I want! Got that?"

Alexis' arm went around Jessica's shoulders. "What do you want?"

His mouth curled. "What you got to offer?"

Her stomach clenched again, and she fought the gag reflex in her throat. "You want money? I have some cash. I can..."

"I want a whole lot of money and more! But first, I'll take that gun of yours."

Alexis swallowed. Could she make the lie believable? "It's in the car."

"The car?" His eyes narrowed. "You had it in your purse before."

"My purse is in the car. I left it there."

His face twisted, but as he started to say something, her phone's ringtone began to play. She grabbed for it, but Leland knocked her back into Jessica.

"Don't touch that!" He picked it up from the end table and pocketed it. "Stand up. Both of you." Alexis shoved Jessica toward the bedroom. "Run, Jess!"

Leland jumped, grabbing Jessica's arm, and yanked her against him. He dug the revolver into her side. "No one's running anywhere!"

Jessica's face paled, and Alexis froze. Surely, someone had heard Jessica's scream before or the commotion going on now. *Please, God, if you're there, let someone call the police.*

Leland crooked his head into Jessica's neck. "At least I left your mom alive. You might not be so lucky."

The girl's eyes rounded. "What are you talking about? What did you do to Mom?"

He laughed. "Wouldn't you like to know?"

"If you hurt her—"

The gun moved, jabbing into the girl's side again. "What? What would you do?"

"She's done everything for you. How could you—"

"Stop whining." He thrust her away from him and looked at Alexis. "And any more stuff from you, and you won't live to see tomorrow. If you don't want Jessie hurt, you'd better do as I tell you. You hear me?"

Alexis nodded. She shot a quick glance in Jessica's direction. The girl's countenance had changed, her expression hardened.

"Now pull that chair over here." He indicated a high-backed chair in the corner.

Alexis walked over and closed her hands around the top spools. She glanced at Leland.

"I wouldn't, honey. You might think you're fast but not faster than a bullet." He laughed as she set it down close to him. The gun's barrel moved and aimed at Alexis' chest. Her breath caught. "Sit in the chair, Jessie, and don't try anything."

Jessica's glare didn't alter as she sat. Leland dug into his jacket pocket, pulled out a length of rope, and tossed it at Alexis.

"Tie her to the chair."

Alexis didn't move, and the man's brow creased. She shook herself. *Don't freeze. Think!* Leaning over, she picked up the rope from the floor.

"You know the cops are looking for you." Alexis bent over the girl. "You should be heading out of town. Not hanging around here."

"Shut up!"

She glanced at him. "You're just making things worse. Why don't you—"

The barrel moved to Jessica. "Okay. Getting rid of her will make the plans I have for you easier."

"No!" Alexis shouted. "No, I...I'll do whatever you say. Just leave her alone."

"Then shut up and tie her in that chair."

Alexis swung the rope around the girl and the chair.

"And do it good. Don't try anything!"

Alexis nodded, swallowing, wondering if she could somehow make it loose enough for Jessica to get free later. When she leaned over the chair, Jessica muttered in her ear.

"What if he hurt Mom?"

Alexis looped the rope again, keeping it loose.

"I'll kill him if he hurt Mom."

"No talking!" Leland took a step forward.

Knock. Knock. Knock. All three of their heads jerked around. Alexis caught her breath. Someone was at the door. If she screamed...

"Don't say anything!" The words hissed at her, and he waved the revolver. "You hear me? Don't say anything!"

The knocking came again.

They stood frozen. The knock became insistent.

"Alexis! Open up. Your car's here. I know you're in there. We need to talk."

Her heart jumped. *Luke!*

Leland signaled with the gun, catching her look. She stared at him. He'd kill them anyway. Whatever his plans were, he couldn't afford to leave them alive. If she was doing to die, better now than being raped and killed later.

"Luke! Get the police! Get—" The gun came across her face. Pain splintered and surged across her cheek. She reeled backward, crying out.

"Alexis?" Luke's voice jumped. "What's wrong? What's going on in there?"

Leland turned toward the door, hand shaking, and aimed. Jessica screamed even as the gun cracked.

Luke's yowl of pain sent Alexis surging toward Leland. He aimed again, and she threw herself at him. The revolver flew from his hand, and they tumbled to the floor.

Chapter 16

Leland scrambled to his knees, lunging for the gun; but Jessica landed on top of him, beating him with her fists.

"You leave my mother alone! Do you hear me, you leave her alone!"

He rolled onto his back, knocking her to her side and cuffed her across the face. When she jerked back, he clambered to his knees and dove for his firearm again.

Alexis surged to her feet, and Jessica leaned across her, grabbing a heavy statue from the end table, but blocking Alexis. Leland's fingers closed around the gun, and Jessica swung the statue toward his head.

Leland shoved a hand up for protection, and his revolver flew free again. He cursed as it skidded across the wooden floor and disappeared under a chair.

Alexis dove after it. The sound of struggling followed her and then a crash. She shoved her head and arm under the chair. Light flashed off the gun's barrel, and she grabbed for it.

Something slammed into her side, and pain exploded through her. She curled in shock, gasping. Hands caught her clothes and dragged her backward. Leland then dropped onto his belly and reached for the gun.

Alexis struggled to her knees, holding her side, nerves pulled tight as catgut. If he got the gun… She threw herself on top of his legs.

The living room window shattered. Alexis yanked her head around. Glass rained across the carpet and the sofa.

Luke slammed the car jack against the window again.

"Alexis! Get your gun!"

As Leland pushed farther under the chair, she jumped to her feet and sprinted for the bedroom.

She grabbed her purse, ripped the zipper down, and snatched the pistol from its holster. The next instant, she stood in the doorway.

Jessica straddled Leland's back. He shoved himself free from the chair, reached up, grabbed the back of her neck, and tossed her forward over his shoulder. Clutching the revolver, he lurched to his feet.

Luke smashed the window a third time, and Leland whirled toward him.

Alexis yelled, and the man spun back around, gun rising. She squeezed the trigger, the pistol jerked, and a loud pop echoed through the room. Leland grabbed his shoulder. His eyes widened, his face scrunching in pain. He thrust the gun in her direction. Alexis fired once more. Leland clutched his stomach, half-turned and dropped to the floor.

Her heart hammered in her chest, deadening all other sound. She stared at the crumpled figure until Jessica's movement caught her attention. The girl pushed to a sitting position. Luke waved from the window, pointed to the front door and disappeared.

The scream of sirens made it through the fog of shock around her. She lowered the semi-automatic. Banging on the door startled her. She took a step toward the door and glanced across at Leland. He hadn't moved. Her body began to shake, and the gun hung heavy in her hand. When the banging came again, she set the gun on the end table, stepped into the hall and yanked open the door.

"Luke!" She threw herself at him.

He caught her with one arm and held tight. "It's okay, darling. It's okay." She buried her face against his neck, and his hand trembled as it touched her hair. When he pulled back, his eyes questioned her.

"I'm okay." She had to force the words. The sound of the

sirens grew. She pushed away and dropped her gaze. "You were hit. Where—"

"A graze. Just my arm." He glanced at his blood soaked sleeve. "Don't worry about it. You—"

The sirens' squeal filled the condo. Flashing red and blue lights strobed the walls. In a moment, the sirens stopped. Everything went quiet.

"Pro...Professor Jergenson?" Jessica's voice sounded strained.

Luke frowned, dropped his arm, and pushed past her to stop abruptly at the room's archway.

"Jessica?" Alexis stepped beside him.

Luke's good arm whipped out and shoved her back into the hallway. "Stay behind me."

The command and the action, as well as what she'd seen, sent a rush of adrenalin through her. On the other side of the room, near the big picture window, Leland leaned against the wall. He held Jessica to his side, his gun in her midsection.

"Let her go, Leland." Luke's voice held a calm authority, the professor giving instructions to be followed.

"Not likely. She's right where I want her."

Alexis' heart seized. She started forward, but Luke's arm rose again, stopping her.

"The police are here." Luke nodded toward the window. "Let her go."

"I'm going to kill her."

"You're not killing anyone. You have nothing to gain."

Alexis' gaze slid to the end table a few feet away. Her gun sat in plain view.

"Bring the pretty girl out. I've got a score to settle with her. Then I might let this one live."

"No."

"Luke," Alexis whispered. "My gun's on the table. I can get it."

His head turned fractionally. "No."

She bit her lip. How could she stand here and do nothing?

Her eyes focused on her pistol again. If she could get to it, if someone distracted Leland for a moment...

Luke's head moved toward the window a second time then back. "You're bleeding all over. Your only hope is to get to a hospital. Give it up, and let her go."

Jessica made a whimpering sound, and Alexis watched the blood drip from Luke's arm to the floor. Tentacles of fear twisted inside her.

God, if you're real, help us.

Beating on the door broke the numbness. "This is the police! Open up!"

"I have a gun and a hostage." Leland's ragged voice barely reached her.

If she tried to let them in, no telling what he'd do to Jessica. "Luke, I don't think they heard him."

Luke's head turned. He cleared his throat and shouted, "We've got a hostage situation here. There are four of us inside. One has a gun."

Movement at the doorway ceased. Alexis eased her head past Luke's arm. Outside, two police officers stood behind their cars with guns drawn. Others moved behind them

Leland gripped Jessica with his good arm, his revolver clutched in his hand. He dragged her closer to the window and glanced out, leaving a track of red stickiness behind him.

More police cruisers arrived behind the others. An officer with the bullhorn lifted it. "Okay. We understand you have hostages, but no one needs to get hurt. We can work out a solution." He waited a moment. "Does anyone need medical attention?"

"Tell them I'm going to kill her."

"He says he's going to kill her." Luke's voice was a shout.

Could they hear him? Even with the broken window... The policeman with the bullhorn lowered it and said something to another officer who walked hurriedly away. The officer turned back their way.

"I repeat – no one needs to get hurt. What do you want?"

Luke shifted in the doorway. "An ambulance is pulling in now. If you drop your gun and go out, they can help you."

Leland yanked the gun up and pointed it at Jessica's head. "No one's going to help."

Jessica's face paled.

"Hold on!" The officer's voice came again, "Let the girl go, and the others; and we'll work something out."

"No!"

Alexis' breath caught. They could see him and Jessica. Hope caused her heart to beat faster.

"Let's talk this out. What do you want?"

"I don't want anything!"

"Okay. I can understand that. If you don't want anything, something must have happened."

"Something happened all right." But the man's voice was low. He scowled across at Alexis and Luke.

"You have a phone?" The megaphoned voice came again. "It will be easier to talk over a phone. What's your number?"

"I said no!" Leland swiveled toward the window and leveled his gun at the man.

Alexis leapt for her pistol, grabbed it and swung toward Leland. He whipped back around, pulling Jessica in front of him. Alexis yanked her hand up, fear slicing through her. She'd almost shot Jessica. Leland grinned and lowered his gun.

Something hit Alexis like a linebacker sacking a quarterback. She crashed to the ground, even as the shot reverberated throughout the room. A second gunshot followed, and something else thumped the floor. She lay still. Quiet settled. The weight of another body pinned her down, and the smell of cordite drifted to her nostrils.

A loud boom came from the door then another. Convulsions ricocheted through her. A series of repeated booms followed, and the door splintered.

"Police! Hands up! Police!"

Her eyes focused on the arm resting against her head.

Luke's. He'd tackled her. She cleared her throat, trying to talk over the shouting and stamping of feet around them.

Someone knelt beside her. "Who's bleeding?"

Alexis tried to move, but Luke's body lay across hers. She could barely breathe. She cleared her throat again. "Luke? Let me up. Luke?"

He didn't move.

Chapter 17

Night had crept in and closed the day by the time the hospital and the police released them. Alexis left the Jag at her condo and drove Luke home in his truck. She'd followed the ambulance to the hospital. Afterward, she drove them both back to her condo to get his truck.

"You can't drive home with Demerol in your system. Besides your arm's hurt, your side's bandaged." He tried to argue, but she put out her hand for the keys. "Your truck's no different from John's, and I've driven that. I'll drive you home, and call John to come get me. Give me the keys."

Amazingly, he'd given in without further argument.

On the way, she placed the call to John and explained what had happened. Would he come to Luke's and take her home? She smiled at his reaction. She wouldn't be able to keep him away. But it would take some time for him to get from the cabin to Luke's, and that was good. She wanted time with Luke, needed time to wind down, to sort things out.

She made Luke sit while she brewed the coffee and put sandwiches together, pulling things from his refrigerator like she lived there. When she sat down, she studied him. He had to hurt; he'd refused more of the Demerol.

"I don't like the narcotics," he told the nurse. "If I can do without, I will."

Alexis swallowed a second bite of ham and cheese sandwich and knew it would be useless to force a third. Every part of her body ached, and it did not want food. She lifted her coffee cup and stared across at Luke.

The crease between his brows and the bandage on his arm

testified of his discomfort, not to mention the bandage she couldn't see under the scrubs he'd worn home from the hospital. Leland had managed to get a shot off before being killed by the police sniper. Luke had caught Leland's shot when he'd taken Alexis down.

She shuddered. Another flesh wound, a narrow escape. The thing that kept returning to her mind was that this God he talked about must have been with him, with them all, today.

Her eyes met his. "I was petrified."

"When? Or should I say which time?"

"When you didn't move."

He gave a lopsided grin. "I was trying to man it out. Didn't want to yell. Took a minute to move or say anything."

She shook her head, and her mind went back to the hospital. "Jessica did well, didn't you think? After all she's been through."

He finished the bite of sandwich in his mouth and nodded. "Yes, especially with all Leland's done to her."

"Done, but won't do anymore. When Jessica dropped to the floor, the policeman outside had a clear shot."

"And took it. We were blessed. A number of the officer's were SWAT team members. They didn't have time to suit up, but carried out their jobs, anyway." Luke ate the rest of his sandwich. "She's an amazing girl. I was proud of her."

"Jessica? Yes, she is. She really went after Leland, too, before you got there." Alexis tilted her head. Amusement rose. "When Leland mentioned Dawn, that was his mistake. The girl got mad. Don't mess with her mother. She jumped him, beat on him and hit him with a statue. We might both be dead if she hadn't been so aggressive. And he laid into her, too, punching her, throwing her over his shoulder. I was afraid she might miscarry."

Luke's brows rose. "Did they say anything about that?"

"The doctor said he thinks the baby will be fine. I hope he's right."

Luke reached across the table to take her hand. "God has a

purpose for that little one. We don't see it yet, but he does."

Alexis studied him. "You think so?"

He nodded. "Yep." Quiet settled around them for a moment. "Now when Jessica saw her mom..."

"I know. She almost cried." Alexis clenched her jaw. The woman deserved to be in jail. She drew a circle on the table. Luke said nothing.

Finally, she looked up again. "Dawn insists she didn't know where Leland was, but I think she's lying."

Luke's gaze held hers. She didn't know whether to cry or scream. *Even though Leland was dead, and Dawn in the hospital, things didn't seem finished.*

Luke's chair scraped the floor. He put his cup in the sink. "What are you thinking?"

"That this wouldn't have happened if Dawn had told the police where Leland was. They would have arrested him."

"And he would have posted bail. Leave it, Alexis. It's not worth the aggravation."

She knew it was true, but..."I want to be angry at someone."

"You shot Leland. Twice. That sounds like angry to me."

She heard his amusement and frowned. "But I didn't kill him. He grabbed Jessica." She dropped her head in her hands. She'd shot him, but he'd almost killed Jessica. If the police sniper hadn't taken him out...

Luke moved, standing so close she felt his breath. "Let's go into the living room."

Alexis stared at the floor. She had wanted to be here with him. That was part of the reason she'd insisted on driving. She hadn't wanted to be alone, hadn't wanted him to be alone. Maybe he'd let her stay the night again, on the sofa in front of the fire.

Alexis raised her eyes to his. His look held so much emotion that it startled her.

He touched her cheek. "Somebody had already called 911, and I did, too, before I got the *jack*; but I felt helpless. I'm not used to that. In the war, we knew what we were up against. We'd trained. We were prepared. But you... When he shot through the door, I guessed it was Leland. But if he was that desperate, what would he do to you?"

"I heard you yell, but I didn't know how bad you were hit."

He glanced at his arm. "More surprise than anything."

"Your side..."

"I'll live."

She put her head down. "I almost got you killed."

"Leland tried to shoot you. I got in the way. His fault. Mine. But not yours." He drew her up from the chair and into his arms. "But you have a problem following orders. I said no about the gun."

She drew her head back to look at him.

The amusement did nothing to cover the other emotions playing across his face. "I didn't want anything to happen to you."

"It didn't."

"Almost."

She put a finger to his lips. "It didn't because you were there, because you knocked me down."

"Because God was there." He caught the hand at his mouth. "Let's sit in the other room."

She nodded and let him lead her into the living area. He lowered himself onto the sofa in slow motion. His face scrunched.

"Luke?" She leaned over him. "You're wincing."

He avoided eye contact for a moment, then winked at her and pulled her down next to him. The quiet enveloped them. The fireplace had no fire. She missed its warmth. Inside, her body felt cold, and she began to tremble.

"Hey." Luke shifted to see her better. "You're shaking."

"Reaction, I guess."

He pulled a throw from the back of the couch and wrapped it around her. "I'll get the fire."

But before he could rise, she buried her head against his chest, not wanting him to move. She was safe here. She'd always been safe with him.

God, I've judged all the men on the planet because of what two did to me. I'm sorry.

Her eyes jerked open, and she stared into his shirt. She'd just prayed again. How many times had she prayed today? What had happened? Did she believe? Had Jessica's talk, all their talks, convinced her?

The assurance they had could be hers if she wanted it, and she did. She wanted the new life they hinted at, wanted deliverance from her own judgmental attitudes, and wanted to leave the past in the past, even if it meant forgiving those who had mistreated her. Could she do that? Could she leave justice in the hands of this God they talked about? Jessica's confidence had stirred her. Releasing them from her vengeance, giving it into His hands. Could she do that?

God, I want freedom. If I could put the past behind me and move on. I've lived in fear and anger for so long. I want to start over. I don't understand everything, but if you'll take me, I'll take you. And accept Jesus' sacrifice for my sins like Jessica said.

The shaking stopped. Warmth filled her body.

"Alexis?"

She glanced up. Luke's eyes were inches from hers, and his mouth settled on hers, gently moving, probing. In a moment, he raised his head, searching her face.

"I need to say something." He waited until she nodded. "When you told me you weren't a Christian, I was so shocked that I exploded. I'm sorry. You didn't deserve how short I was with you that day. I didn't listen to what you had to say, didn't try to understand. I just blew up and left. Will you forgive me?"

"Yes. It's okay."

"No, it's not. I hesitated about becoming involved with you...well, because you're a lot like Teresa." He moved his hand. "No, wait. You're not, actually, but at first… You're an attractive woman, Alexis. Teresa was, too. She couldn't handle…me. Didn't want the whole package."

"You were right that second time. I'm not like her."

"No, you're not. Not in ways that count. And I know it sounds crazy, but when you said you weren't a Christian, it was just another way for you to leave like she did."

"Luke, I didn't leave. You left."

He winced, but she wasn't sure if it was the pain or her words.

"I did. I shouldn't have expected you to understand what that meant to me since you weren't a Christian." His mouth twisted. "And that is what's most important. Jesus. Will you let me tell you about Jesus?"

"But I…"

"He's more important than anything that's happened. And a relationship with Him is the best relationship you can have. He's a man you can trust. He loves you more than I or anyone else could."

"Luke, wait. I—"

"He's real, Alexis. If you'll just study the claims the Bible makes. Matthew, Mark, Luke and John are testimonies – just like you'd get in court – eyewitness accounts. If you'll study them like you would any case—"

She put her fingers on his mouth again and stopped him. "I just did."

"You did what?"

"Whatever you call it. Accepted Jesus. Said okay to him, to God."

"You did?" His voice inched up. "When?"

"Just now. While you were holding me. Just now."

"Just now?"

She laughed. "Yes, just now."

"But…"

The pounding on the door stopped them. They both glanced around and said at the same time, "John."

❦

Alexis sat on the edge of her bed. John had scooped her up from Luke's place after a short discussion and taken her to her condo – reluctantly. He wanted her with him and Sharee, wanted to make sure she'd told him the truth about being okay. But she needed time alone. Only she hadn't reckoned on the state of her condo. The management or a compassionate neighbor had boarded up her window, but blood had congealed on the floor, on the window sill and other places. John helped her clean, and both his anger at what she'd been through and his comforting presence massaged her soul.

He tried once more to get her to go home with him, but she refused. Jessica was at the hospital with her mom, and Alexis had the condo to herself.

The strange warmth that had descended at Luke's house still hovered. She clasped her arms over her midsection. Something had disappeared from inside her, something dark and heavy. Light permeated her insides – light and lightness. Saying she felt buoyant didn't describe it, but she could think of nothing else.

Except maybe freedom. Does this have to do with you, God? Who are you? And Jesus? What am I supposed to do now?

She glanced at the nightstand and at the Bible on it. Scooting over, she picked up the book and thumbed through the pages. Where to start? John had always told her to start in the New Testament at the Gospel of John. Easy to remember he'd said and grinned. Well, she'd done some reading there the other night, trying to run down Luke's references to this new life he talked about. But she'd started somewhere in the middle of the chapter reading about the woman caught in an adulterous situation.

They'd dragged her to Jesus, expecting him to condemn her; but he hadn't. After they all left, he told her to go and sin no more. So, he didn't condone what she did, but he hadn't thrown stones at her either.

This man, Jesus, had more to him than she realized. Courage and strength and fairness. She liked him.

Moving to the chair in the corner of her room, she thumbed through the book once more, put her finger on a page and stopped. John 2:19 on the left side, John 4:38 on the right. She let her focus travel over the small print. Some in black, some in red.

"In reply Jesus declared, 'I tell you the truth, no one can see the kingdom of God unless he is born again.

"'How can a man be born when he is old?' Nicodemus asked."

Alexis settled back in the chair. Now that would certainly be a new life. Being born again. How would Jesus answer this?

Chapter 18

Luke heard her car just as Farley raised his head. "Stay, boy. It's okay."

He moved from the kitchen to the living area, glanced out the front window and watched her walk to the door – the late-riser surprising him with a visit before full sunrise.

So much had happened last night that his feelings had coagulated in his chest. However, he still wanted this morning what he'd wanted last night – for her to find Jesus. She said she had, but had he understood correctly? Was it real?

He said nothing, just backed away from the door and let her walk in.

Why is she here, Lord? They hadn't had another chance to talk after John arrived. Luke ran a hand through his hair and shoved his tiredness aside. He'd taken the few hours of sleep he should have had last night to wonder and pray about where they'd go from here.

The moment of silence brought a smile to her face, highlighting the long bruise on her right cheek. He wanted to touch it. The fire of anger burned briefly, but the man who had caused the bruise was dead. That part of their story was finished. What would the rest hold?

"You still have that flavored creamer?"

He nodded. "Of course. Yes. Come in."

She walked ahead of him into the kitchen, sat in her usual chair; and he went to get the coffee and creamer.

"I couldn't sleep," she said.

"I wondered how you would cope."

"I could have slept here with the fire going."

He didn't know what to say to that. That situation would have proved dangerous. He shoved the picture of her sleeping on his couch out of his mind. The picture from that first night gave him trouble at times.

"So, I had to come early—"

"Alexis." He cut across her words.

"What?"

"Did you mean what you said last night?"

"About God?"

"And Jesus."

"Yes."

"Truth?"

"Luke, my life is built on truth. Because I strayed one time trying to help myself and the college doesn't mean I'm a consummate liar."

He set the cups on the table, filled them with coffee and put the creamer in front of her before sitting across from her. His fingers rested on her hand. "I know."

Still, he'd wanted to be sure. His heart, which had sat frozen with uncertainty all night, began to beat.

She stood abruptly and walked to the window. He stood, too. Should he say more? He wanted to. How would he say it? "Great. You're a Christian. Let's get married." Somehow, he didn't think that would work. She had to know how he felt. He'd opened himself up to her last night. What if life with him was not what she wanted?

"Alexis."

She didn't turn. Her profile was beautiful. The modest jeans and loose shirt didn't hide the curves beneath. He loved looking at her. *But what did she see in him? What was there to see?*

He'd failed at one marriage already, and marriage, for him, meant lifelong commitment. Or it had. And it was still what he wanted. Only he wanted to do it right this time. He wanted her...holding her in the morning, eating breakfast, riding together, laughing, discussing their work…

Only, it would kill him if she said no or if it didn't work. Still, he had to know, one way or the other. "Alexis, why are you here? Why are you bothering with me?"

She turned from the window. "What?"

He waved at her in a way that indicated her whole body. "What is someone like you doing with someone like me?"

"Because I like you? Because there are no dull moments around you? I don't know. Why? What are you asking?"

He waved at her again, heart sinking. *Like?* "You're one of the most beautiful women I know, and I…well…" He cleared his throat. "I'm plain. I'm an amputee."

"Plain?" Her eyes rounded. "Plain? There's nothing plain about you."

"I'm not handsome, not by today's standards. I have one leg."

"A leg and a half." She moved across the room, invading his space. "You are a little rugged looking – like you've seen too much." He frowned at her, and she laughed. "You have great eyes and a character face. No, it's not exactly handsome, but I've never thought about it. And we've already discussed the leg issue. If you can deal with it, I can."

She liked him, she'd said. Like wasn't what he wanted.

"Pretty women want pretty men."

"Luke, it was Teresa's loss, her hang-up, not yours. Let it go."

He frowned again and took a step back. "It wasn't just her hang-up. It was me. I changed."

"Yes, and I'm glad you did. You know the outside is just the outside, and it's what's inside that counts. 'Whited sepulchers' Jesus called the Pharisees. I read that the other day and laughed myself silly. Jesus had a way with words. They were religious bigots. Pretty on the outside, full of dead men's bones on the inside. If I had an accident tomorrow, if I lost a leg or an arm, would you drop me like a hot tamale?"

"No. You know that."

"Of course I know that. Let's get past this then. Besides, you're gorgeous the way you are."

Gorgeous? Now she was lying again.

She stepped into his space once more. "It's not important to me what a man looks like. You should understand that. What's important is his heart." Her finger tapped his chest. "Your heart. Your gorgeous heart. People get old, people change. Some have accidents. If all you have is a face or a body, then you have nothing permanent. You, of all people, know that."

He took another step back. "No one said anything about permanent."

"Yes, they did."

"No, they…"

"I did."

"I tried permanent before." Why was he fighting this? It's what he wanted, what he'd been thinking.

"Not with me."

He felt her scrutiny; his was as intense. She was the gorgeous one, and he loved her. Could she possibly care as much? Would she stay?

She drew her head back. "Don't tell me I'm too pretty."

After a moment, he lifted a corner of his mouth. "That was my thought."

"And don't take another step back. You'll crush Farley's tail."

He dropped his head, glancing behind him. The dog lifted his. Luke turned back to find her face six inches from his. Heat radiated from her. *Whoa.* His heart kicked up a notch. Her fingers trailed over his jaw, and his breath deepened.

"It doesn't matter, Luke. I'm not here to score points with the world. I'm here because I love you, because I thought you loved me. What's important about someone is what's inside."

She loved him? His eyes focused on hers, searching. His heart slammed against his chest.

"You love me?"

"Yes."

"You do?"

"Yes."

He slipped an arm around her, pulling her close. The erratic up and down of his heart caused him to grin. "I love you, too."

Alexis tipped her head back, studying him again. "I thought so. You love me and what else?"

"What else?"

"You love me, *and...*"

Her finger tapped his chest, and the light poured inside as it had the day God filled the weight room with His presence. He'd let the assurance God gave that day slide. Now he felt it pouring back. Leg or not, and, ultimately, Alexis or not, he was okay.

"And?" His brows rose, wondering what she wanted.

"We were just talking about it."

It took a moment, and then his grin widened. "I want permanence, too. With you. Lifetime. Family. Permanence. Will you marry me?"

A smile broke out on her face. "Yes. Yes. Yes."

Before he thought, his mouth had covered hers; but she pushed into him, into the kiss. He drew back in surprise, holding her away.

"Alexis, I'm no saint."

She chuckled. "You think that's news?"

"I mean I'm no priest. Do you know what you're saying? Yes to marriage?"

Her face became serious. "Of course, I do." Her hand lifted to his jaw again. "I trust you, Luke. I trust you to be gentle and patient. And now, I trust God, too."

He groaned at her words, at the faith they implied, at the beauty he saw inside her and knew that God had given him far more than he'd asked or deserved.

I hope you enjoyed reading ***Looking for Justice.***

Authors need and appreciate book reviews.

Could you please take a few minutes

to put a review on Amazon?

Amber Alert is a prequel *to Looking for Justice.* The next couple of pages will give you a peek at this romantic suspense novel due out this fall.

Amber Alert

*A Christian Romance
with Mystery and Suspense*

December, 5:00 am

How many people does it take to find a baby?

Sharee Jones sent up the desperate plea to God, even as her body protested the long, wet search. Exhaustion and discouragement, enhanced by the cold December night, increased as darkness turned toward morning. Her flashlight illuminated the muddy ground, and she leaned a shaking hand against a tree. Those on either side of her stopped. Sounds from other searchers echoed through the darkness. Their lights, whispered voices, and the moonlight imparted a surreal feeling to the area.

How many people does it take to find a baby? A small regiment, Sharee realized. Now that the Amber Alert had gone out, the police, dog handlers, church members, neighbors, even strangers from across town had joined the frantic battle against time.

She raised her arm into a narrow wash of light. Her watch glinted. Eight hours since the baby's disappearance. The chances of finding him – and finding him alive – faded with each sweep of the watch's hands.

Now and again, she glanced back. The Christmas lights from an enormous six-pointed star pierced the darkness, mocking her. Peace on Earth, good will to men? Could there be any peace until they found Joshua?

Her best friend's child had vanished, and it was Sharee's fault. She'd planned the program; she'd agreed to Joshua's part in it. An infant playing the baby Jesus. It had sounded wonderful, and since the mother and father also volunteered to play Mary and Joseph, well...how much better could it get? Or so she'd thought.

Sharee closed her eyes, her heart fracturing, and then the image of that first mutilated doll burst across her mind. Her eyes flew open. Kidnapped... or worse.

She slipped on the muddy ground, and a man's hand reached out to steady her. His other hand shot upwards and grabbed a wet branch as it snapped back at them. Cold rain splattered their faces. Sharee pulled free, wiped the rain from her eyes, and glanced at John Jergenson. He rubbed a hand across his own face and caught her look. She ducked her head and turned away.

"Ted, we're right behind you." John's voice didn't have the exhausted quality Sharee knew hers did, but stress echoed in his words. "Watch the flying branches, will you?"

"Sorry." Ted Hogan's answer drifted back from the darkness ahead.

Sharee stared at the place from which Ted's voice materialized. Her beam held both pines and underbrush in an unearthly glow. Vines twisted upward, catching on anything in their way. She thanked God that Ted had joined them a short while ago. A four-person team worked better than three. She and John and Lynn Stapleton had headed out as soon as they received permission from the deputy. When Ted arrived later, thankfulness welled up within her. They needed all the help they could get.

Earlier, the sheriff's deputies had searched the church buildings and the grounds and found nothing. This undeveloped land next door had acquired major importance. Other groups were wading through the trees and brush, while some inspected the nearby pond and the stand of cypress. Officers had canvassed the neighborhood.

A gasp from behind startled her. She glanced over her shoulder. Lynn's long, blonde hair hung soaked and dripping, except for one strand caught in a long-fingered branch. Her gunmetal, quilted parka glistened with moisture, and mud covered the stylish high-heeled boots. Lynn yanked the hair free.

"You okay?" Sharee shoved a hand through her own wet hair. Her jeans and sweatshirt offered no better protection against the elements than her friend's clothing.

"I'm okay. Just wish I had something to pull this back with." Lynn wrapped the waist-length hair around the top of her head once more. "If I had a clip—" She stopped and her eyes widened.

Sharee jerked around, shooting her beam across the dark foliage in front of her. Lights and faces floated, ghost-like, among the trees before emerging into features and visages she recognized. She let out a long breath.

"We're going in for a while," Pastor Alan Nichols said, stepping from the darkness. "Come with us."

Ted appeared from the gloom behind them. "Go in? No way. We can't stop."

"No one's giving up. It's been a long night." The pastor nodded to two soaked individuals passing them. "We all need a break and something warm."

"Go ahead." Ted's voice hardened. "I'm staying. I got here later than the rest of you. Besides, Ann doesn't need us quitting."

"We're not quitting." The pastor moved aside as a third person went by him. "But we all need to dry off and get something to eat. Daybreak's an hour away. They'll be forming a line of searchers then, covering the same ground we've covered tonight." He glanced at Sharee and Lynn and sent a frown John's way before following the others.

When John's focus settled on her, Sharee straightened and picked up her chin. He let his light play over her then swept it over Lynn.

"Alan's right," he said. "We need a break. Ted, help Lynn. Those boots she's wearing weren't made for this mud."

"I'm fine," Lynn said, teeth chattering.

"And I said I'm staying." Ted's voice grated.

"You can't stay." Sharee grimaced at the roughness in her own voice. "The deputy told us to stay in groups of three or four."

"I don't care what he said."

"They don't want anyone out here alone, and you don't want to go through another interrogation, do you?"

Ted muttered under his breath, but a moment later he grasped Lynn's arm. Sharee's heart gave a strange blip as she slipped past John's outstretched hand and headed back.

Too much tonight, Lord. Too much.

When they reached the open field forming the church's boundary, they dropped onto the nearby bleachers. Other search groups sat together, speaking in whispers. Some had cups of warm liquid in their hands. Steam rose like small ghostly apparitions from them. White lights from the enormous star that stretched parallel to the ground and eight feet above it added another eerie glow to the night.

Where was Joshua? Who had taken him? Sharee stared past the lights into the night shadows. God's presence and the joy it had infused in her throughout the Christmas program last night had evaporated.

How could this happen, Lord? How?

Silence filled her heart. She bit her lip. Her fault. Her best friend was in agony. Joshua had disappeared, and it was her fault. She shoved wet curls from her face. Her body shook.

John stepped next to where she sat on the bleachers. She could feel his scrutiny, but avoided his eyes. He lowered himself beside her, and his fingers feather-touched her hair. She swallowed, resisting the urge to turn to him, to bury her face against his shoulder.

After a moment, he straightened, and she followed his gaze to the second set of bleachers. Ryann Byrd, surrounded by a number of other teens, huddled on the top row. Of course, she needed support. She'd been through so much already.

Sharee noticed another figure at the far end of the bleachers. Deputy Richards, feet spread and arms crossed. He stared up at Ryann, too. Then he turned, his gaze flickering past each huddled group until they reached Sharee. He looked from her to John and back again, and in the light from the Christmas star, she saw his eyes narrow.

Author Biography

Linda was born and raised in Florida. She is married with two grown sons, a daughter-in-law, and three grandchildren. At twenty-six, she discovered the miraculous love of Jesus. God blessed her with a passion for the written word—especially mysteries and romantic suspense novels, from Nancy Drew to Agatha Christie, from Dee Henderson to Kristen Heitzman.

She speaks about and works against human trafficking. She blogs on this subject and on commitment to Christ at *www.lindarodante.wordpress.com* (Writing for God, Fighting Human Trafficking).

To learn more about her books, this series, and the author, please visit *www.lindarodante.com*.

Authors need and appreciate book reviews. Could you please take a few minutes to put a review on Amazon?